CITY OF GOLD

BOOK TWO OF ELEANOR MASON'S LITERARY ADVENTURES

NIKKI MITCHELL

POISON APPLE
PRESS

City of Gold

Poison Apple Press, LLC

This book is a work of fiction. Any names, characters, and places are a product of the author's imagination or are used fictitiously. Any resemblance to actual events or people is entirely coincidental.

First edition: March 2021

ISBN: 978-1-7348985-1-4

Map by William Marcell

Cover design by Hina Babar/FM by Faemance

Editor: Jennifer Navarre

Librarians across the world—this one's for you.
You help bring stories to life in the minds of young readers.

This one is especially for my favorite librarian, Dale Safford.

City of Gold

PROLOGUE

The evil imp shall unleash the gold
The news shall travel to the enchantress of old
Meet the girl where the sun shines bright
And she will save you from this destructive plight.

E leanor stood at the top of a hill, looking down at a field of golden wheat. At first, she thought it was just normal wheat, probably part of a farmer's crop, but then something about it caught her eye. The sun was incredibly bright, so she squinted, looking hard at the tips of the plants. They glittered. It was the same sheen as if the sun's rays were hitting pure gold.

"Of course, this is not a normal field," Eleanor said to herself.

She looked around to see if she could see anyone in the distance, but there was nothing except for the magical wheat. With a deep breath, she started running through the tall plants, just like she had done in fields of soft grass and daisies in the summertime back home. Eleanor loved feeling the soft tips of the wildflowers and expected to feel the same here, so she outstretched her hands, forgetting that these were not the fields back home.

Her fingertips grazed the wheat, and Eleanor immediately pulled her hands back in. She stopped and looked at her fingers. They were bleeding. She wiped the blood on her pants and looked at the wheat. She reached out with one of her uncut fingers and lightly touched the tip. It was pure gold.

Eleanor looked around again and found herself surrounded by a sharp crop, burning hot in the sun.

Eleanor Mason, as you know from the *Nightshade Forest*, was given a super special fairytale book that transported her directly into the story. It was a Christmas gift from her father, who worked at a printing company. The first time she read from the book, she disappeared into the Nightshade Kingdom, without her parents even noticing she was gone, which caused her to be very curious about how the book worked. While inside the story, Eleanor quickly discovered that she had taken on the role of a main character and had to do whatever she could to save the kingdom in order to return back to her tiny home in Michigan.

After saving the day in the Nightshade Kingdom,

befriending two fairies, and returning home just in time for Christmas pudding, Eleanor carefully set the book on her shelf and returned to her normal activities of schoolwork, chores, and reading *Alice's Adventures in Wonderland*. It was the start of a new year, 1946, and Eleanor's father had been working later shifts at the printing company.

A few weeks had passed, and Eleanor's parents had said nothing about the magical book, or the fact that she had completely disappeared for days in the book realm, and just minutes in the real world. Before opening the book again, she wanted to understand its magic a little bit more.

More than anything, she was curious to find out if Pix had traded places with her while she was in the book.

E leanor saw her mom making lunch in the kitchen and pulled up a chair to join her. She sat before a bowl of boiled eggs.

"Did you have any visitors on Christmas?" she asked, grabbing an egg that still felt a little warm.

"Visitors?" her mom asked.

"Yeah, you know, any other little uh…girls?"

Eleanor's mom wiped her hands on her apron and turned to look at her daughter.

"What little girls would be coming to visit?"

"I don't know. Maybe a cousin." Eleanor avoided all eye contact with her mother.

"Well, dear, I'm not sure who you saw in our house, but it was definitely just the three of us, unless you count the carolers that showed up in the evening."

Eleanor scooped up another egg and thought for a minute. Maybe the real Pix had shown up as Eleanor.

"Was I acting weird at all?"

"Not that I remember, but you're acting a little

strange now," she said with a curious laugh. "Is there a reason for all of these questions?"

"I—I was just curious." She put the half-peeled egg back in the bowl and ran into her room before her mother could ask any more questions.

Once in her bedroom, Eleanor carefully closed the door and paced in front of her shelf. She tried to think back on that day, but she only remembered sitting in the same exact place as she had left—next to her parents on the sofa. Maybe Pix didn't go anywhere, she thought. Maybe because it was a work of fiction, Eleanor just dropped into Pix's character.

Eleanor looked out her window and saw the snow falling in heavy batches. Her father wouldn't let her help outside today, and her mother never gave her any extra chores on Saturdays. She looked back at her shelf and carefully picked up the little book with the charred cover. Eleanor had so many questions, and there was only one place in town that might have the answers she was looking for. She grabbed her burlap sack, set the book inside, and slipped back into the kitchen.

"Mama, is it alright if I go to the library today?"

"Are your chores finished?"

"Inside, yes. I don't think Papa will ask for help in the woodshed today with the blizzard."

"It is snowing pretty heavily out there, dear. Are you sure you want to go out?"

"It's just the next block over," she pleaded. "I promised Mrs. O'Leary that I would come see her soon, and I haven't been to the library since before Christmas."

"Alright. I guess you can go, but please be careful. If the winds are too strong, I want you to come back inside."

"Yes, Mama."

"Oh, and will you see if they have any new herb books in?" she asked.

"Sure. I'll be back in a little while," Eleanor said.

"Would you like some lunch before you go?"

"Nope, I'm not hungry." Eleanor already had her boots and wool coat on. She whipped the scarf around her neck and disappeared out the front door.

2

The wind blew against Eleanor and snow slapped her in the face as she fought her way to the public library. While it was only a block away, the weather made the trip much longer—and much colder. Michigan winters were long and cold, and she hoped the next story she landed in was somewhere warm and sunny.

She kept her head down for most of the walk, but as she saw the sidewalk cleared, she knew she was getting close. She looked up and a smile appeared on her face. Just the sight of the grand staircase, marble lions, and stained-glass windows on the large mahogany doors made her heart bang against her chest. It wasn't quite like the library in the Nightshade Kingdom, but it was a magical place. She knew there had to be some book on the shelves that explained magical storybooks.

The wind fought her when she tried to pull the door open, but Eleanor gave it all of her strength and snuck in the opening before the door slammed shut. A loud *thud* followed, and Eleanor took in the smell of the books and wood polish that filled the room. She waited for her eyes to focus in on the dimly lit lobby and headed for the circulation desk. Mrs. O'Leary, the librarian, was usually sitting behind the desk with her nose in a book, but today, her chair was empty.

Eleanor reached for the little bell and the sound echoed through the entire room, followed by a crash from behind a door just behind the circulation desk, with a sign that read STOCK ROOM. Eleanor cocked her head just slightly, as the M was hanging sideways. The commotion worried her a bit, so ignoring one of the rules neatly written on the sign in front of her, she stepped over what she imagined was an invisible line and headed for the door.

Just as she was getting close enough to call out, the door flung open and a flustered woman in a crocheted afghan, winged glasses, and a disheveled smile appeared, making sure the door was shut tightly behind her.

"Are you alright?" Eleanor asked, focusing on the seven pencils the woman had stuck into her tightly wound bun.

"Ah, Eleanor dear. Yes, I am fine. You gave me a startle with that bell. What brings you here on such a blustery day?" she whispered.

"Just looking for something good to read," she said.

Mrs. O'Leary always had the best suggestions for books. For the longest time, Eleanor thought she lived at the library because she was the only one there, even late into the night. She was even sure that Mrs. O'Leary had memorized the location and title of every book in the building.

Sometimes her husband, Mr. O'Leary, would be lurking around fixing things. He always insisted on everyone calling him Hank though because Mr. O'Leary was too formal. Eleanor made a mental note to remind him about the M on the sign behind the desk the next time she saw him.

"Would you like me to show you the newer books today, or did you have something specific in mind?"

Eleanor was about to speak when she felt the book in her bag start to move. She looked down and used one finger to pry open the bag just enough to peek in. The book was trying to get out.

"Your dad told me he found you your very own copy of *Alice's Adventures in Wonderland*. Have you gotten through that already?" Mrs. O'Leary asked.

"Oh yes. It's my favorite," Eleanor said, looking around the room for a section that was out of sight. She couldn't have anyone finding out about her magical book. At least not until she did some research first. "Do you know if you have anything on magical books?"

"I'm not sure what you mean, dear." Mrs. O'Leary glanced toward the room she had just come from, almost like she was double checking that the door was secure.

"It's…hard to explain. I'll just look around, if that's okay with you."

"Take your time. But I am closing at three o'clock

because of the weather." Mrs. O'Leary attempted to straighten her hair and found her place behind the big desk.

"Okay. Thanks, Mrs. O'Leary." Eleanor smiled and took a left to the nonfiction section. She grabbed the bag a little tighter.

Eleanor found nothing on magical books after briefly browsing, so she decided to look at the fairytales section. She hoped she could spot a book that looked similar to her book. She grabbed a stack of Grimm's fairytales, a few by Lewis Carroll, and some other fairytales that she had never heard of before.

She looked around for a large table and saw that her favorite one, the one near the large fireplace, was empty. She rushed toward it and spread the books out. She sat down, carefully setting her bag by her feet, and warmed her hands before grabbing the first book.

She started with the first Grimm's fairytale book she had pulled off the shelf and thumbed through the pages. She loved library books because they always had the prettiest pages, many of them filled with gold leaf. The book was similar to Eleanor's magical book, as it was filled with different stories, ranging from princesses to a creepy guy named Rumpelstiltskin.

She paused when she saw the rough sketch of a small guy sitting next to a spinning wheel. She read the little scribbles underneath and quickly turned the page when she read that he had tried to kidnap a baby in return for the gold he had spun.

"Glad that's not in my book," Eleanor said with a shudder.

The time ticked by as she browsed every book she could find, but nothing mentioned a magical book. Eleanor looked around to make sure Mrs. O'Leary wasn't anywhere near before pulling out her book. She set it down next to the others, and just like the books in the Nightshade Kingdom library, it shuddered. Eleanor wiped her eyes and looked at it again to make sure she wasn't just tired from staring at pages all afternoon. It shuddered again. The book wanted something, but Eleanor didn't know what. It hadn't done this at home at all.

She thought about it for a moment and wondered if this book had originally come from a magical library in some other world. Maybe it belonged there. She thought that maybe…just maybe…there was another kid like Eleanor who had traveled between worlds and brought the book back. She wasn't sure how it ended up in her dad's printing company, but it definitely didn't belong in this world.

She heard footsteps and shoved the book back into her bag.

"Any luck, dear? I'm about to close soon." Mrs. O'Leary gave Eleanor a suspicious look after seeing the titles sprawled across the table.

"Yes, I think I will borrow this one," Eleanor said, scrambling. She picked up the book closest to her, which happened to be one of the Grimm's fairytales.

"Okay, just bring it to the front when you're done, and I will get it logged for you." Mrs. O'Leary gave her a quick smile and left.

Eleanor scooped up the rest of the books and put

them back on the shelves. She didn't have any interest in checking books out today, but now she had to. She double-checked that her book was still tucked safely into her bag and walked to the front desk.

While she was filling out the card to borrow the book, Eleanor looked around at Mrs. O'Leary's desk. She saw a couple of plants and remembered her mother.

"Oh no!" Eleanor said.

"What is it, dear?"

"My mom asked me to check out a book on herbs, and I completely forgot."

"Oh, I think I have a few back here that Mrs. Wells returned this morning. Will any of these do?"

"Oh, they are fine. I'll take them all," Eleanor said, hoping that at least one of them was what her mother was looking for.

Mrs. O'Leary pulled the tattered cards from the back of each book and slid them across the desk for Eleanor to sign and date. Then she neatly printed the return date in the books and passed those to Eleanor.

Since it was nearly closing time, Mrs. O'Leary led Eleanor to the main doors so that she could lock them once Eleanor was on her way back home.

"Stay safe out there and tell your folks I said hello. Those books are due back in a week."

"Thank you. See you next week! Tell Mr. O'Leary hello for me." Eleanor rushed out the door. She gripped her bag to her chest, not wanting it to blow away. She pushed herself against the big gusts of wind, but it was no use. Her scarf blew off of her neck and she didn't have time to catch it. She had to get home before the storm got any worse.

Eleanor turned and looked over her shoulder and saw Lake Superior's waves crashing over the rocks. Stronger winds were coming. She tightened her grip on her bag and started to run, watching out for patches of ice.

3

Eleanor pushed through her front door and a wave of snow followed her in. Her mother had come around the corner with a basket of linens and frowned when she saw the snowy mess on the floor.

"I'll clean it up, Mama. Sorry. It's really bad out there."

"Well, I'm glad you made it home safely. What did you find at the library?"

"Oh, just another book of fairytales," she said, clutching her bag a little tighter. "And your book of herbs."

Eleanor reached into her bag and handed a thinly bound book on edible plants and two books about harvesting herbs to her mom.

"I hope that's what you were looking for," she said, taking her coat and boots off.

"This will do," her mother said as she quickly swept the snow back out the door. The wind caused the door to fly open, and Eleanor's mom had to pull hard to get it to close.

"Do you still have any lunch?" Eleanor said. Her stomach quickly reminded her that she hadn't eaten since breakfast and there was still some time before dinner.

"Sure. I'll make you a sandwich," she said.

Eleanor hung her coat up, took her sandwich, kissed her mother on the cheek, and rushed into her room.

She closed her bedroom door and plopped down on her feather mattress. Eleanor opened her bag and dumped out the contents. She tossed the library book on her bed. The Grimm's fairytales bounced as it hit the mattress. Eleanor's attention was strictly on the book from her father. She held it in her lap, watching it intensely, waiting for it to move.

When nothing happened, she tapped its cover, almost expecting a reaction. Nothing happened.

"Was I seeing something?" she said in a whisper, flipping the pages. No, she had felt it moving too.

She looked around the room. Maybe it was reacting to other books, fairytale books. Eleanor grabbed the library book and set it next to hers. It didn't budge.

She looked at the clock on her tiny desk: it was a quarter past three, and Mrs. O'Leary was gone for the day. She let out a deep sigh. With this weather, the library would be closed for at least one day for snow clean-up.

Eleanor vowed to go back as soon as the library

opened again, but for now, she figured she could get some answers from inside the book. Remembering how hungry she was the first time she vanished into the book, she decided to eat lunch first.

Eleanor quickly ate her sandwich and ran her fingers over the charred spine of her book.

"One, two, three," she said in a whisper before opening it. The gold leaf had been burned off, the pages were wrinkled, and it smelled of smoke, but it was a book that Eleanor would never give up. If she were right, and it had belonged to someone else, or somewhere else, she had no idea why they would have given it away.

She turned to the table of contents and found her treasure from her last adventure. The purple leaf she had brought back from the enchanted forest was still very much alive, to Eleanor's surprise. She twirled it by the stem a few times, smiled at the adventures she had with Elfie, and vanished into the second story: *The City of Gold.*

4

Eleanor carefully walked through the wheat until she finally found some resemblance of a path, keeping her hands locked at her sides. Her fingers still throbbed, even though the bleeding had stopped. After studying the path, she quickly realized that it wasn't a man-made trail, but a deer trail. She had seen several in the wooded areas back home. She was curious as to how animals managed to creep through the field without getting torn apart.

As she walked deeper into the field, the stalks seemed to get taller, until they were the same height as Eleanor. Her mind wandered to her adventures with Elfie and Milo, and she was wondering if today would include any wolf chases, when a noise behind her made her jump.

She carefully turned around, expecting to see another person, but instead the noise came from something close to the ground. Eleanor used her hand as a visor and looked down. It was hard to focus on anything because of the glare from the sun and the gold. Finally, she saw a brown rabbit with gold-tipped ears.

"Did she send you?" it asked, looking directly at Eleanor.

Eleanor's eyes grew wide and she stooped down closer to the rabbit. "Excuse me, did you say something?"

"Yes, yes. I asked you if she sent you!"

"Who?"

"The enchantress," he said, hopping in circles. The rest of his ears quickly turned gold.

"I'm not sure what you mean. I am sorry. Can you tell me where I am, please?"

"Oh dear, oh dear. This is not good. Not good at all." He hopped faster, and the gold spread again.

"My name is Eleanor. Can I help you in any way?"

"No, no. Not Eleanor. This is not good." His ears were now completely golden and stiff. "The enchantress was supposed to send Lilura to help us. The prophecy said so. I was supposed to meet her where the sun shone the brightest so she could save our city."

Eleanor looked to the sky and was blinded. The rabbit seemed to know what he was talking about, as she had never seen a sun so bright before. She knew she must be the girl that the rabbit was speaking of, and she had to at least try to keep her cover. With Elfie, she had come clean early on, but she really wasn't sure if the rabbit could handle the truth right now.

The rabbit eyed her nervously.

"Oh, this was part of the test," she said. "I'm not able to reveal my identity to just anyone. I had to make sure you were someone who had heard the, uh, prophecy," she told him.

Eleanor looked down at the rabbit. The fur on the very top of his head had turned too. Whatever the problem was, it was spreading quickly.

"Can you tell me what I need to know?" she asked the rabbit. "What is your name?"

"I am Fenek."

"Okay, Fenek. Can you let me in on what has happened so far?"

"He has turned the whole city to gold, and soon all of the wild creatures of the city will turn as well," he said, pointing to his ears.

"Oh dear, that isn't good at all," Eleanor said. "Who would do something like this?"

"We do not know his name," Fenek stuttered. He looked to the sky, as if something were going to come snatch him up and take him away. "He once worked for the king."

"You don't know his name?" Eleanor asked, shocked.

Fenek looked nervously at the sky again. "No."

"How is that possible? Everyone has a name," Eleanor said, confused.

"There is rumor that it begins with an 'R,' but that is all we know. It is impossible to know if he has never revealed it."

"Could it be Ronald? Or Roland? Or—"

"His name does not matter. There are more troubling things at hand," Fenek said.

"Oh right. You said something about a prophecy?" she asked.

Fenek motioned for Eleanor to bend closer, but instead she picked him up and he whispered in her ear.

"I can't tell you here. I will tell you somewhere safe."

"Does it at least say how I save the city?"

He looked at her with concerned eyes and shook his head. Gold specks flew into the air. "Why did the enchantress send someone who does not know? We don't have time! Oh dear, oh dear."

"Oh, don't worry. I will figure something out," she said, her stomach churning. She continued to carry Fenek through the path. The giant stalks came to a stop and Eleanor had to cover her eyes at first, because everything was so bright. After a minute, she uncovered them and squinted into the distance. Just down another hill sat an ornate city. Normally she would expect hints of gold for decoration, but every building was pure gold.

"I can't be too late; this is just the first chapter," Eleanor said to herself.

Eleanor remembered the Nightshade Forest and how her character there had belongings and magical power to help her save the kingdom. She realized then she didn't even know what her character looked like. She had learned in the first story that appearance affected her abilities, and this time, she found herself wearing thin black pants, a cotton tunic, and black-

and-white sneakers. She also had a small pouch around her stomach, which she quickly unzipped. After reaching inside, her hands grasped a pair of sunglasses.

"Ah, these will help a lot," Eleanor said.

She continued to rummage around the pouch and found two small vials. One was labeled *Lilura* and the other *Fenek*. Eleanor's curiosity grew when she saw that the vials held a mysterious silver liquid. She pulled the stopper from Fenek's vial and held it up to her nose. It smelled of fresh flowers and spring. She was about to put the stopper back in when she noticed Fenek's ears were even a deeper gold. She held it over his head and let a drop spill onto his fur. Instantly, the gold disappeared, and he was back to normal.

"Oh, thank you, thank you!" he shouted.

"Glad to help. We'll just keep the rest of this safe in here," Eleanor said, dropping the vials back into her pouch. With her sunglasses on, Eleanor's vision became clear, and she knew there was no time to explore this city—she had to find a way to stop this unnamed person. She decided to start calling him R.

"Fenek, do you know where he is right now?" Eleanor asked.

"Oh yes. He is in the high tower," Fenek said, pointing to the giant gold palace.

"I thought this was a city. Why is there a palace?" Eleanor asked.

"Many, many years ago, a king ruled this place. He was an evil man who hired this evil imp to be his sorcerer. The terrible king was starving his people. All food was delivered straight to the palace, and the townsfolk had to figure out their own way to eat. People started going underground and planting food the king's guard didn't know about. Bakers would smuggle loaves of bread into the underground markets and claim that some loaves had burned too much for the king's taste."

As she listened to Fenek's story, Eleanor hoped that she wouldn't have to face the king too. He sounded worse than Prince Franco and the grumpy dwarf combined.

"He raised taxes, and a small group of people started an uprising," Fenek continued. "At first, the uprising started as whispers in the underground markets. Shopkeepers were upset because the king paid them less and demanded more. The food and goods they were able to bring into the markets started to dwindle, and starvation was looming over everyone."

"Then what happened?" Eleanor asked. Fenek was such a great storyteller, she had forgotten where she was for a minute.

"Soon, the whole kingdom came against the king and all of the royals. The women and children were safely secured underground, and the rest of the townsfolk marched toward the castle."

"Did they at least try to talk to the king? Ask him to lower the taxes and demand less goods?"

Fenek shook his head. "The king wouldn't listen to anyone other than his sorcerer. Some say the king had lost his mind. Some say the power went to his head. Nobody really knows. But no amount of pleading would help."

"What did they do once they got in? Did they capture the king?" Eleanor asked.

"Before the mob broke through the palace gates, the king and his sorcerer disappeared. They were never seen again. It is legend that the king died of old age, but as a sorcerer, the imp will live forever."

"So, after the king left, a new king wasn't selected?"

"Oh no, no, no. The townspeople came together and decided they would run the city together. Too much power is no good."

"Alright. Does R have any guards we need to watch out for?"

"R?" Fenek asked.

"Yeah, that's what I am going to call him."

Fenek shook his head. "He doesn't need guards. He has a giant crow," Fenek said, nervously looking around at the clouds.

"Okay, well, let's go talk to some of the townspeople. You be on the lookout for the crow."

5

The city sparkled, and everything was extremely bright, even with Eleanor's sunglasses. Fenek hopped nervously behind her, looking to the sky every few seconds.

Eleanor looked around, noticing that all of the houses had their shutters closed and no one seemed to be out and about.

"Where is everyone?" Eleanor asked curiously.

"The enchantress didn't give you much information, did she?" Fenek asked.

"No, not really, but we do need to talk to some of the villagers," Eleanor said, wishing she had more than just the vague prophecy and Fenek's information.

"Everyone mostly keeps inside now that he has taken over. But some do hide in the Bird's Nest Café."

"I guess that's a good place to start," Eleanor said. "Lead the way."

She followed Fenek through the gold cobblestone

path. She looked around, wondering how many things R had turned gold, and how much was originally gold.

"So, when did R show up?" she asked.

"Oh, his crow has been watching for a while, but the town didn't start turning gold until a few days ago," Fenek replied.

He continued the story as he led Eleanor down a dark, twisted street. He explained that just R's presence in the town had bewitched the buildings, and then soon after, the wheat had turned to gold. Farmers were in an uproar because the metallic crop couldn't be harvested, which meant no grain for the bakers. While the gold was worth a small fortune and could pay the rent, the fear of starvation was too much.

The road began to twist and turn even more, and Eleanor took off her sunglasses because it had gotten really dark. She noticed the path clearly led to a dead end. She looked up and saw a tattered wooden sign swinging from above the door of a creepy building.

The building looked to be brick at one point in time, but pieces were either falling off or had already fallen off. The windows on the second and third floors were boarded up, and even with no sun, a weird shadow was cast over it.

"There, there!" Fenek said, pointing at the exact door Eleanor was hoping wasn't the Bird's Nest Café.

"That's where the townspeople gather?" Eleanor asked.

"Oh yes. He won't find us here. It's a secret place," Fenek said, raising his eyebrows.

Eleanor tried to open the door, but it wouldn't budge. "Um, Fenek, how do we get in?"

"You must know the secret knock."

"Can you show me?"

"Rap three times with the knocker, call three times for the doctor, tap twice with a finger, and pretend you're a singer," Fenek whispered.

Eleanor let out a snort. "No, seriously."

Fenek gave her a puzzled look.

"Another riddle? Really?" she asked, frustrated.

"I am the keeper of riddles. Rap three times with the knocker."

Eleanor lifted the heavy raven-shaped knocker and let it knock on the door three times.

"Call three times for the doctor!"

"Doctor, Doctor, Doctor!" Eleanor said, embarrassed. "This is ridiculous."

"Tap twice with a finger!" Fenek said, ignoring Eleanor's comment.

She did as Fenek said and was dreading the last part of the riddle.

"Now pretend you're a singer."

"Why is this necessary?" she asked, wondering if Fenek was just messing with her.

"The door will not open if you do not finish the knock."

Eleanor let out an "ahh-ahh-ahh." She expected her normal, rough voice, but a perfect melody came flowing out of her mouth. Lilura could sing!

The door swung open, revealing a dusty, low-lit

room. Eleanor entered and Fenek hopped happily after her.

"Oy Fenek! Where've you been?" asked a scruffy man behind the counter. He had a beard that went on forever.

"Oh, hi Brutus. I was just finding my friend," Fenek said, hopping up onto a stool. He motioned for Eleanor to come sit with him.

"And who's this friend you've brought us?" Brutus asked, sliding a giant piece of cake and a steaming cup of tea to Fenek.

"Is this carrot?" Fenek asked, pointing to the giant sweet on his plate.

"Would I give you anything else?" Brutus said, turning to Eleanor. "What will it be, dear?"

Eleanor's stomach rumbled. She looked at Fenek's plate and admitted that it looked delicious. Her mother would have never let her have a piece of cake that large, especially without lunch first. Then she remembered the sandwich she had eaten earlier. Her mom would be fine with it; she was sure of it.

"I'll take what he has, please," she said.

Brutus laughed. "You don't want what he has. That cake is for the creatures. It tastes pretty awful." He disappeared into a back room.

Eleanor looked at Fenek, who was shoveling cake into his little rabbit mouth like crazy. She looked around the tiny room and noticed that most people were hunkered down in the corner booths. The tables in the middle were completely empty. Nobody spoke above a whisper. She wondered if this was how it usually was, or if it was because of R.

Brutus came back through the rotating door with a piece of brilliant red cake with white icing and topped with a handful of mixed berries. Eleanor's eyes grew wide. She had never seen a cake so beautiful before.

"Will this do?" Brutus asked, smiling at Eleanor.

"Oh yes," she said, scooting closer to the counter.

"So, what brings you here? I thought everyone had heard about our, uh, company and fled."

"Fenek found me and asked if I could help."

At those words, Fenek blurted out "Prophecy" with his cheeks stuffed full of cake.

"Ah, you're the girl from the prophecy Fenek has been carrying on about for the last few days. I don't quite believe in 'em myself, but if you can help, you can help. Got any ideas?"

"I might, if Fenek would actually tell me the prophecy," Eleanor said, looking at the rabbit, who was now gulping his tea to wash down the cake.

Fenek did a quick scan of the room with his mouth still stuffed with bits of cake. Nobody other than the three of them seemed to be close to the counter. He swallowed one last gulp of tea, set his fork down, and motioned for Eleanor to come close.

She leaned in, almost falling off of her stool, but Fenek motioned for her to come even closer. Eleanor hopped down and stood right next to the rabbit.

"The evil imp shall unleash the gold

The news shall travel to the enchantress of old
Meet the girl where the sun shines bright
And she will save you from this destructive plight."

"I could have told you it myself. I've heard it at least once a day for the last few days," Brutus said.

Fenek gave him a disapproving look and pointed to his empty glass.

Brutus grunted, filled Fenek's mug, grabbed a rag out of a bucket filled with dirty water, and began cleaning the counter.

Eleanor repeated the prophecy over and over in her mind but came up with nothing. It was so vague.

"Fenek, are you sure that's all of the prophecy?" she asked.

He looked at her and nodded his head. "Yes. That is all. But the enchantress always trains her girls to be prepared for all prophecies. Her girls are trained in their powers to distract. Your voice, your ability to change your appearance. You're the sirens of land."

"My voice? I'm supposed to save the city with my voice?" Eleanor chuckled, but then remembered the few notes she belted out to get into the café. Maybe Fenek was right. But who would be distracted for more than just a minute with a pretty voice? Unless it was magical. She sat back on her stool.

"Yes, yes," Fenek said with cheeks full. He gulped down the big bite before continuing. "Your presence will be a surprise. You'll show up and sing, and that will stun him enough for you to take control of the wheel."

"Yeah, I'll think about it some more," Eleanor said, taking another bite of her cake. She wasn't convinced. But still, she played the riddle over and over again.

After what seemed like ages, Eleanor's mind couldn't focus on the riddle anymore. She looked around for a place to curl up for a nap. It was so dark, warm, and cozy in the Bird's Nest, she didn't want to leave. Her eyes were heavy.

With half of the cake still on her plate, she dropped the fork, letting it hit the edge of the plate with a soft *cling.* Her head rested softly on her arm.

6

Fenek was too busy enjoying his snack to even notice Eleanor's plight.

Through hazy eyes, she saw Brutus come in and out of the back door to deliver the red cake to others in the café. On his way back from delivering a plate, he noticed that Fenek was nearly finished with his cake, so he swooped around to the other side of the counter.

"Can I get you another piece, my friend?" he asked Fenek.

"Oh no, but thank you. I think Lilura and I are going to go find a quiet booth and talk about our plan to save the city." He glanced over at the girl, only to find her just about asleep.

"Lilura! Oh dear," Fenek said, seeing Eleanor with her head on the counter. "Lilura, please wake. We have a mission. Oh no." He hopped up on the counter and shook her awake.

"Just a few minutes, please. I am so sleepy."

Fenek looked around and saw the reason it was so quiet.

"Why isn't anyone talking?" he muttered.

Like Eleanor, everyone had fallen asleep after eating the red cake. He looked nervously at Brutus.

Brutus caught Fenek's eye and shrugged his shoulders. "I gotta do what I gotta do to make a living. You understand, don't you. He wants the whole place asleep so he can finish his plan. He said all of the people had to sleep, but the creatures had to stay awake. I didn't ask questions. He paid me in gold, Fenek. Pure gold. Don't look at me like that. I was going to lose this place."

"Oh dear. Oh dear. The prophecy said nothing of a friend's betrayal."

He nudged Eleanor again. Her eyes were only half-open.

"Brutus, you will lose this place anyway, if we don't stop him. Of course, he promised to pay you in gold; he is making the stuff outside of town! Next, he will pay you in a golden rabbit, if we don't do anything about this. I don't know what he promised you, but you can never trust a sorcerer."

"Alright. I'll make you a deal—if you don't tell *him* who did it. If I help wake her up, will you leave and tell everyone you know not to come here? I don't want to put anyone else to sleep, but I had to make a deal with him. You understand, don't you?"

"No, oh no, I do not. I do not want your help. I will wake her on my own." Fenek continued to shove on Eleanor's shoulders. "Please, Lilura. Wake up!"

He looked back at Brutus. "I shared the prophecy with you. Did you tell *him* what it was too? Is he expecting us?" Fenek's whole body shook in fear.

"Hey, I wouldn't have done that," Brutus said.

The panicked Fenek looked back at Eleanor, defeated. Then, he remembered her pouch. He climbed down onto a stool and opened it. He rifled through its contents, finding a shiny silver whistle. He blew it into Eleanor's ear, and she sat up abruptly.

"I'm sorry, Fenek, I just couldn't seem to shake this sleepiness," she said, rubbing her eyes.

Brutus shook his head and disappeared into the back.

"We have to go. He paid Brutus to put all of the humans to sleep. It's part of his plan. Please, let's go before he comes back," Fenek said, hopping toward the door.

Eleanor shook herself awake and followed Fenek. "Wait, what?" Eleanor had heard everything, but it hadn't sunk in until now.

Fenek repeated what he had said, and Eleanor's mouth dropped open in a half-yawn, half-exclamation.

"Is that why I was so tired? Did Brutus poison me? Was it in the cake?"

"Oh, not poison. Just sleeping powder, I am sure. And yes, the cake contained it."

"I should have had a Caesar salad instead," Eleanor said.

They reached the door and Eleanor looked back to the counter, but Brutus was nowhere to be found.

"I'm not sure I like your friends, Fenek."

"Brutus is a nice man. It's just the times," Fenek said. "Everyone is petrified, and gold is hard to pass up."

"Fenek, we need to stop R. Everyone will be asleep soon. People are fleeing to the Bird's Nest for safety, but it's not safe anymore. He has found everyone. How is he turning everything gold? Is he using magic?"

"Oh, the wheel. The wheel is magic. As long as he has gold wheat to spin in the wheel, it will turn whatever he asks it into gold."

"How did the wheat turn gold?" Eleanor asked, remembering the unending supply she saw when she first landed in the city.

"Legend says that the king granted R one wish as his sorcerer before they fled. But whenever a sorcerer is separated from his king, his magic is void. The king told him that all he had to do in order to make the wish come true was to return here and ask the fountain fairy. She's a statue now but was once an actual fairy. She grants wishes and prophecies with the toss of a single gold coin. I'm sure that this was his wish."

"Take me to her," Eleanor said. "She may finish the prophecy for me, if I toss her a coin."

"Okay, but his crow will be watching. He watches all day until the stroke of midnight."

"Why midnight?" Eleanor asked.

"Midnight is always when the new day begins. It's the time that sorcerers always work on their evil plot. The sky is darkest, the moon is brightest, and shadows are lurking."

These words sent chills up Eleanor's spine.

"So, is it just a normal crow?" she asked, thinking about the birds that often picked at her garbage or on roadkill left on the side of the road.

"I'm not sure what a normal crow is," he said, puzzled.

Eleanor had forgotten that she hadn't spilled the beans to Fenek. Normal crows would just be crows in this world.

"Oh yeah. I mean, is it a special one since he belongs to R?"

"I have never seen a crow this big," Fenek said, looking to the sky. "His wings are huge and dipped in crimson. I think he can see through walls."

"Will my voice keep him at bay?"

"Unfortunately, we creatures are immune to your… uh...powers."

"Well, we will wait then, until midnight. Where can we stay until then?"

"My home is always welcoming to friends," Fenek said, nervously eyeing the sky.

"I would love to see where you live," Eleanor said, relieved that she had some company here. Plus, she knew she had to encourage the nervous rabbit if she wanted any help stopping R.

7

Fenek's hole was more than Eleanor had ever expected a rabbit to have. It was hidden in a grove of bushes and had a small orange door. When he opened it, the smell of the deep earth hit Eleanor. Ducking, she followed Fenek through the hole in the hill. After a moment of adjusting her eyes, she saw a very small cellar. The whole place reminded her of her potato cellar back home.

A soothing aroma filled the home. It reminded her of a special tea her mother would sometimes make to calm her nerves, with chamomile flowers, orange peel, and honey for a little sweetness. When she was really nervous about something, or just not feeling well, her mom would add an extra bit of orange. Eleanor breathed in this lovely reminder of home. For a moment, she had even forgotten the fate of this fictional city rested upon her shoulders.

She was pulled back into reality when she heard the clang of dishes.

"Would you like some tea?" she heard from somewhere over in the corner. The voice sounded much like Fenek's, but he was standing right next to her. She looked around, trying to figure out who was speaking.

Finally, she saw the tips of gray ears. She looked closer and saw a rabbit a little smaller than Fenek viciously stirring a cup of tea.

"No, I think I am fine for now, thank you," Eleanor responded. She looked at Fenek. "I didn't know you were expecting company."

"Oh no, not company. He is my dad."

Before Eleanor could say anything, Fenek hopped over to the other rabbit.

"I will have a cup of tea, Pop-Pop."

"Oh good, yes. I counted the minutes. I thought you were turned to gold. You have the girl, yes? As the prophecy said?" Eleanor tried to eavesdrop, but the rest of what he said was in a ramble.

"Is he okay?" Eleanor asked.

"Oh yes, he is fine," Fenek said, trying to stop his face from turning any pinker.

The rambling continued, climbing in volume. Eleanor caught "doorstop" and "lost forever," but that was it.

"Are you sure?" she pried. "He doesn't seem okay."

"The keepers of prophecies eventually go mad," Fenek said, hanging his head. "It is too much. Too much for one mind."

Eleanor moved closer to Fenek's dad. In the low light of the candles, she could see he had a long, fluffy mustache and was wearing a monocle. He was exactly how she would picture an older rabbit…in a fairytale, that is. She felt bad that his mind was lost in riddles. He continued to ramble in rhymes as he added heaping spoonsful of sugar.

Eleanor studied him for a little bit and wondered if Fenek would share his fate.

"Actually, I do think I will take a cup of tea, please and thank you," she said with a sad smile. This was her first time in their home, and she didn't want to be rude.

"Oh yes. Three scoops or two?" he asked, still stirring.

"Two, please." She turned to Fenek. "I think we should devise a plan and then get some rest before midnight."

"Very well," Fenek said, hopping into the living room. "Come sit."

Eleanor was surprised how much room Fenek had managed to create in such a small space. His living room was filled with wooden furniture covered in plush pillows. A small fireplace sat on the far end of the room, and Eleanor felt right at home. In fact, she wished she would never have to leave until she was ready. But R was trying to destroy the city.

Eleanor looked around even more before finding a place to sit. Over in a far corner sat a small stool and table. The wall above the table had been written on, but Eleanor didn't understand what it was.

Fenek caught her staring and explained. "He tries to get the prophecies out of his head, to solve them, even if they are not his."

"Will he be okay?" Eleanor asked.

"Yes. He just keeps to himself in our hole. He makes the townspeople quite nervous. They don't like the muttering all the time. Plus, a lot of townsfolk think that the prophecies bring bad luck, and if you are the bearer of one, only ruin will come with you." Fenek seemed to get lost in his mind, but quickly snapped out of it. "But he is helpful here," he said, motioning to his cup of tea. "One will always find the perfect cup of tea here. And the fire is always stoked. Plus, he helps me figure out the ones in my head too."

"Aren't you afraid to give him more?" Eleanor asked.

Fenek climbed up onto a chair made out of a hollowed-out log and sipped his tea. "It is our job."

"But why?"

"I'm not sure. It just is," he said.

Eleanor peered into the kitchen to see if her tea was ready, but she saw the rabbit sound asleep with the teas on the counter. She didn't want to disturb his rest, so she stayed with Fenek, who hadn't noticed anything different.

"Well, you know more about this city than I do, so I'll need your help," Eleanor said, changing the subject.

"Oh yes, I know I am to help. That is why the prophecy came to me," he replied.

"I sure hope there's more to that prophecy when we see the fountain fairy tonight. I'm not sure how to get into the palace and take the wheel."

"Oh no, Lilura, you must not take the wheel. The

wheel is what curses the owner." Fenek's dad had appeared directly behind Eleanor.

> *"He who spins the wheel around*
> *Will pull precious gold from the ground.*
> *For all the spun gold you put on display,*
> *Beware: for a price there will be to pay."*

She jumped, and Fenek eyed her strangely.

When she finally calmed her heart, she asked him to repeat what he had said. Eleanor turned the words around in her mind for a little while before asking her biggest question. She wasn't even sure who to ask, Fenek or his dad.

"First, how do you know so much about the wheel? And how did R acquire the wheel?" she asked, looking at Fenek.

When she turned her attention back to Fenek's dad, he was gone.

"Pop-Pop was stealing carrots from the king's garden when he overheard R tell the king what the fountain fairy had told him. Of course, he had no idea what R was talking about, but the words stuck in his mind. Remember, we are the keepers of the prophecies. Any I hear, stay with me forever, as they do with him." He took another sip of his tea. "I'm not sure how the wheel came to R, but he has been immortal with it. I don't think he has realized the price he will pay."

"What will be the price?" Eleanor asked, staring into the glow of the fire.

"I hope it is that he loses the wheel and disappears for good. Maybe the enchantress will trap him somewhere once the wheel is destroyed. He is untouchable while it is under his control."

"We have to destroy it?" Eleanor remembered that the last time she found herself in a fictional world, she only had to return the stolen property to its rightful owner. "Doesn't it belong to someone?"

"Oh dear, no. The wheel must be destroyed. It belongs to no one; it just imprisons whoever takes control. It whispers to every human, every creature, promising riches and gold. But as the prophecy says, there will be a price to pay. And I imagine that with all of the gold he has spun, and is spinning, the price will be dreadfully high."

8
_____

Eleanor stared at the fire again for some time while Fenek finished his tea. The clank of the spoon hitting the cup caused her to break away from her thoughts, but only for a moment. In the fire, images passed.

"Fenek, why are there creatures moving in the fire?" she asked.

"Oh, that is how creatures travel here. It's the quickest way through different realms."

"There are other realms?"

"You are from another realm. Of course, there are other realms."

"Then why can't we go to another one and get help?"

"The prophecy chose you. There is not another one who could save us."

Eleanor knew the answer to her own question, but it didn't hurt to ask. She looked down at her hands and wondered if she had fire power here too. If that were the case, destroying the wheel would be easy. Wheels were made of wood. Fire burned wood. She'd be home before dinner. She thought very hard of fire, but nothing happened. She even whispered it, but her hands stayed the same.

"Other than the magic from the wheel, is there any other magic here?" she asked Fenek.

"Very old and ancient magic still rests in the kingdom, but it has been buried since the uprising. The townspeople are afraid to unleash it and be ruled again."

"We may need to unleash it in order to destroy the wheel," she said.

Fenek's eyes grew and he shook his head. "That is a dangerous thing to even think about. I told you. You were sent because of your voice."

"How was the magic buried after the uprising?" Eleanor asked, ignoring Fenek's comment. "If we know, we may be able to come up with a plan that unleashes the magic, destroy the wheel, and bury it again."

"We should visit the fountain fairy first."

9

F enek and Eleanor talked for hours about different ways to destroy the wheel, until they both dozed off. Eleanor could very faintly hear the clanking of a teaspoon against porcelain, which meant Fenek's dad must have gotten back to making her cup of tea. Fenek had set the large clock in the living room for midnight, so they could make the trek to the fountain. The loud strokes made them both jump as they came out of their slumber.

Eleanor slowly crawled off of the couch, snapped her pouch around her waist, and took a giant sip of cold tea that Fenek's dad must have brought to her while she slept.

"Alright, let's make our way to the fountain fairy," she said, wiping sleep out of her eyes.

Fenek opened the door and cautiously looked at the sky from the safety of his home. Once he determined it was all clear, he and Eleanor snuck outside. They walked softly through the path that Fenek said led to the main city. Eleanor stumbled on the rocky path. There was light from the full moon and bright stars, but it was hard to see the rocks and roots. Soon, the path had turned into rough cobblestone and Eleanor could relax a little. Fenek had no problem hopping over all of the obstacles.

Golden streetlamps shone brightly as they reached the town square. Fenek motioned to the center of the square, and Eleanor was surprised at how beautiful the fountain fairy was. She had expected an old, crumbling statue stuffed in a dreary fountain. Instead, she saw a tall, marble woman with outstretched wings. She was holding a clay pot adorned with silver crystals. Her eyes were set with emeralds, and jewels covered her marble wings. Eleanor swore it looked like Elfie for a minute, before remembering she wasn't in the Night-shade Forest. In that moment, Eleanor wished she had Elfie with her to help stop R. She'd take wolf chases over an evil imp any day.

Fenek and Eleanor both searched the sky before walking to the fountain. He had been right; R's crow was nowhere to be seen. The town square was eerily quiet, but Eleanor chalked that up to everyone was either too afraid to come out and be turned to gold or had been enchanted by Brutus in the Bird's Nest.

As Eleanor approached the fairy, its wings started to glow. Fenek hopped around happily and whispered to Eleanor, "She has one! Move closer and listen carefully!"

Eleanor reached into her pouch and prayed that it held a gold coin. Relief came over her as she pulled one out. She tossed it into the fountain, and the entire fountain started to glow.

Fenek's excitement died after he saw the lights. "Oh dear, oh dear, he may be able to see the lights from the palace. We must hurry."

She pulled her pantlegs up to her knees and climbed into the fountain. The water was surprisingly warm. The fairy's eyes began to glow, and she began to speak.

"The enchantress' chosen one will succeed.
The sun will rise twice, and the imp will concede.
To destroy the wheel, you must take on a disguise.
Turn the wheel into gold before the sun will rise."

Eleanor tried to concentrate on the fairy's words, but she was soon interrupted by a panicked Fenek. At first, annoyance crept over her. Between Fenek and his dad, they kept interrupting any valuable information she was able to get; she knew she needed to hear the fountain fairy clearly. But then, she heard the warning coming from her rabbit friend.

"Lilura! The crow!" Fenek shouted, pointing to the sky. He started to run down a dark alley, and Eleanor followed closely behind. She looked up and saw nothing. No shadow of a crow against the light of the stars. She stopped to catch her breath, bent over with hands on her knees. Before she had time to figure out her surroundings, Fenek was pulling her toward a door.

"Quick! In here, Lilura!" Fenek whispered loudly, while pointing to a creepy brick building.

"Can we trust this place?" Eleanor said, eyeing the black metal door. "The last place you took me, I was poisoned."

"Oh no, not poisoned. Just sleeping powder," he said, annoyed.

"Right. I didn't realize there was a difference," she mumbled, following the rabbit through the door.

10

Her stomach turned as soon as the stench reached her nose. Inside, there were huge vegetables of all kinds hanging from the rafters. She plugged her nose and ducked under the onions. Eleanor's mother strung onions up in her vegetable cellar back home, and Eleanor hated when she sent her down to collect anything for dinner.

A small bit of light was coming from a bigger room just a bit farther in. Eleanor hoped that the smell of the onions didn't creep in. She couldn't plug her nose forever. Fenek motioned for Eleanor to stay put for a second, and she rolled her eyes. With her nose still plugged, she studied the vegetables hanging from the ceiling. Turnips, onions, and carrots of every color were strung up with a thin twine. "Yuck," Eleanor whispered, expecting her comment to be unheard. Unfortunately, her whisper echoed through the halls.

Fenek hopped back to Eleanor, and her face immediately turned red like the radishes hanging above her. She was thankful that everything was dimly lit.

"One should never insult their host's home, Lilura. It is bad luck," he said.

"I'm just not a fan of vegetables," she said softly.

"Are you a fan of staying safe? She has welcomed us; you should introduce yourself."

Eleanor followed Fenek through the dark hallway into the room at the end. Eleanor immediately noticed that the person who lived here must not be a fan of lights. The room was brighter than the room holding the vegetables, but only a few lamps were lit. Eleanor looked around, trying to find their host, when she saw the enormous armchair by a roaring blue fireplace. Sitting in the chair with a fur blanket over her lap was a very pale woman with long red locks.

"I see the enchantress is still recruiting young girls," she said softly.

Eleanor felt a chill take over the whole room as she spoke. She had a hard time making eye contact with the woman. She didn't quite understand what the woman was talking about, so she just shrugged her shoulders.

"Ah, this is your first mission. I remember mine quite well," she said. "I had to take on a beast who was holding up a whole castle full of people he had trapped through the years."

"So, you are like me?" Eleanor asked. Relief filled her voice.

"I am, except I left the enchantress. I knew my

powers were strong enough to be out on my own instead of doing her bidding. I was her first trainee."

"Oh. So now what do you do?"

"I live a life I love. I grow crops and help the village thrive. The farmers bring me a share of their crops, and I can come and go as I please. I'm not out on impossible missions because of a witch who is too lazy to do it herself."

The word *impossible* swirled through Eleanor's mind, and she felt her knees go weak.

"Don't worry, girl, Fenek always brings me the young ones. The silly riddle will come to pass, and you'll be fine. But I can't seem to put my finger on something. There is something different about you. What is your power?"

"Power? Um—" Eleanor stared at her shoes. "I, uh —Fenek said it was my voice, and my um..." She closed her eyes in defeat. She looked up to see the woman staring at her, waiting for an answer. In an attempt to remove the icy stare, Eleanor blurted out "Fire" and hoped for the best.

"Fenek, why on earth would you bring me an imposter?" the woman asked. Her voice remained calm.

"No, no imposter. I followed the rhyme. I solved the prophecy. She was there." Fenek hopped to the other side of the room, muttering the rhyme under his breath.

"She may have been there, but she is not a true girl of the enchantress." She looked back at Eleanor.

"You're not Lilura. You possess her powers, her name, and her training, but you are not her."

Eleanor felt like she was about to collapse. She was terrified to tell this woman who she was. She could only picture herself strung up like the turnips. One of her hands found the dirt wall, and Eleanor let it hold all of her weight, so she wouldn't pass out.

"Come sit. These powers are tiring you. I must ask myself why on earth a human would take on the powers of a sorceress. We have no magic here, so only your voice and possibly transition powers will work. But they are still in you, for the other realms."

Eleanor sat in the chair near the woman. She didn't even know her name, but she finally took a second to look her over. Her flowing red locks fell just past her shoulder blades. Her eyes were a very powerful blue, and her skin reminded Eleanor of the pasty white plaster on her walls at home.

"So dear, please tell me who you are, so that I can help you."

"My name is Eleanor. I'm—"

Fenek appeared next to her again, whispering "Oh no, no, no, no. Wrong again."

"Fenek, my dear rabbit, be still. Go on, Eleanor."

"I'm from the realm of America, I guess you can say. I have this magical storybook and it takes me into the story." She was about to tell the woman that she could only make it home if she could make it through the last chapter, but she didn't trust her with that information.

"Well, I have seen magic of all sorts, so even

though I have no idea what you are talking about, I will take your word as your honor. What is a book?"

"A book?" Eleanor asked, laughing.

"It is funny?" she asked.

Eleanor calmed herself back down. She didn't need to insult the only woman who could help her get home. "No, I'm sure you have books. They must be called something different here," she said. "They are bound pieces of paper with valuable information written on them."

"Why would you write down valuable information? That information could be stolen and used against you. Or it could transport you into a realm you clearly do not belong in. No, we do not have *books* here. We use riddles here."

"Prophecies," Fenek whispered.

"They're simply riddles," the woman argued.

"So, where do you keep your stories?" Eleanor asked.

"In our minds," she said, confused.

"So, this is a verbal culture. I have read about them."

"In books?"

"Yes, in books. That's how we learn back home. And can I ask your name?" Eleanor asked.

"Claire."

Fenek continued to bounce around nervously, looking between Claire and Eleanor.

"Is there something you'd like to ask, Fenek?" Claire asked.

"I think he wants to know if you can help. We went to the fountain fairy, and—"

"Oh, that fraud," Claire scoffed.

Eleanor ignored her and continued with her story. "She gave us a prophe—"

"Riddle."

"Riddle." Eleanor rolled her eyes. "Anyway, and then the whole place lit up like crazy and R's crow came back."

"R?"

"Oh, yeah, that's what we've been calling him."

"What was the riddle this time?" Claire asked.

"The enchantress' chosen one will succeed.
The sun will rise twice, and the imp will concede.
To destroy the wheel, you must don a disguise.
Turn the wheel into gold before the sun will rise."

Fenek recited the riddle quickly and then looked at the moon out the tiny window. The sky was getting lighter.

"It's almost sunrise," he said. "We need a plan."

"Earlier, you said I had powers and that they were tiring me. What are my powers?" Eleanor asked.

"You possess the voice of distraction, and quite possibly the ability to transform your appearance. Any others are based on your strengths, but they are useless to us here, so we won't even bother."

"So, I could have been right, about fire?"

"Not even close. I'm not sure what you mean about fire as a power, but it is not one in this realm. But I think we need to focus on the real issue. We should call you Lilura while you're here though because I don't think anyone else knows you've fallen into our realm," Claire said.

"Oh, that won't happen," Eleanor blurted out.

"You've done this before?"

"Once, yeah. The real one comes back after I make it back home." She paused for a moment. "I think."

11

————

Claire stood up from her chair and walked toward a stone door, which was opened just a little. She disappeared through the door and came back out with a chest.

"You can use these supplies if you'd like. But tonight, you will sleep here. It's not safe for you outside right now anyway, so you should sleep."

Eleanor looked around, wondering how she would be able to sleep with the smell of onions hanging over her head.

Claire swished her arms in the air and two beds popped down from the dirt walls. "These should suffice," she said. Before Eleanor could thank her, she had disappeared.

Fenek hopped onto the smaller bed and paced until he found the most comfortable spot. Eleanor's mind was only on the chest of supplies, but she knew how nervous Fenek got when it came to breaking rules. So, Eleanor crawled under the scratchy covers on the bigger bed and pretended to sleep. She waited, listening closely to the sound of Fenek's breathing. Once it became shallow and soft, she sat up and looked around.

"Fenek," she whispered.

No response. He was sound asleep. She crept out of bed and made her way over to the chest sitting in the middle of the room. Even with the fountain fairy's riddle, Claire's explanation, and everything else, Eleanor was still confused as to how she was supposed to know which singing voice to use and how she was going to save the kingdom with that. The Nightshade Forest had been easy compared to this one.

Slowly and quietly, she lifted the latches on the chest. The second one made a loud *clunk*, and Eleanor jumped.

She paused and looked at Fenek, making sure she didn't wake him. He rolled over onto his other side, but that was about it. With a sigh of deep relief, Eleanor turned back to the chest. She felt like a pirate, ready to open a whole chest of loot, but this loot carried a certain weight: the fate of the entire city rested on it.

Eleanor held her breath and opened the lid. Inside was a small blade wrapped in a red leather sheath, a few empty bottles that Eleanor guessed once held elixirs, and a bundle of paper wrapped in the same leather that the blade was secured in. She opened the pages and found what Claire had called riddles. Every page had at least a dozen of them, some in English, and others in languages Eleanor didn't recognize. She sat in the middle of the floor with her legs crisscrossed and started to read each one, hoping to find information about the ancient magic Fenek had been so afraid to talk about.

She was so lost in the words on the pages that she didn't hear the door open and Claire come in.

"I knew you were much too curious to wait," Claire said softly behind Eleanor.

Eleanor sprung up, threw the book into the chest, and slammed it shut. Her face matched the red leather around the blade. Slowly, she turned to face Claire, and was a bit surprised when she saw a smile sprawled across her face.

"I—"

"I'd be worried if you weren't," she said. "After all, the whole quest rests on your shoulders." Claire chuckled.

Surprised by the change of mood, Eleanor let a smile creep across her face as well. She quickly glanced over to Fenek, who was still asleep.

"Oh, don't worry about him; he's a nervous Nellie," Claire said, rolling her eyes. "I believe you were looking through the riddles?"

"Um, yeah. Are those all yours?"

"Yes. And ones that I overheard others receiving. I figured they may be of use."

"But I thought you didn't like the idea of writing things down, you know, in books?" Eleanor teased.

"Well, I suppose some things are worth writing down," Claire said, heading to her chair. "So, I'm sure you have questions."

"Oh, so many. I honestly have no clue how I'm going to destroy that wheel."

"If I remember correctly, aren't you supposed to turn it to gold?"

"But how?"

"Here, give me that book. That wheel has been turned to gold once before. I don't know how that imp got it working again, but it has been done."

For the first time since landing in the field of golden wheat, Eleanor felt a shred of hope. She handed the book over to Claire and sat in a smaller chair next to her.

Claire thumbed through the pages, making different faces at each one. Eleanor wondered what kinds of adventures Claire had been on all these years. Eleanor thought about it for a second and was about to ask her how old she actually was, when she realized Claire would probably know about the ancient magic.

"Fenek mentioned some sort of ancient magic," Eleanor said. "But when I asked him about it, he told me that it had been buried and it would be too dangerous to let it loose to destroy the wheel."

Claire looked up from the collection of pages. "He is right on that one," she said. "Even the enchantress couldn't harness it. It almost wiped out this entire realm. Releasing it and expecting it to do your bidding would just be careless."

"But why? Isn't magic supposed to be used?" she asked, frustrated at the lack of answers.

"Some ancient magic came before the people in our

realm. It was only controlled by great sorcerers, and they just don't exist anymore. Besides, magic isn't always the answer. Riddles take brains to solve. Brains. Not magic."

"Well, magic got me here in the first place," she said, forgetting who she was speaking to.

"Yes, and as you can see, you're in a bit of a pickle." Claire looked back down at the pages. "Ah, here we are. Yes. I won't read the silly thing, because I hate rhymes, but you'll get the idea. It was actually a rabbit who did it last time—makes sense," she said, looking over at Fenek. "Probably related to him. Anyway, it looks as though he took a blade after the golden string that attaches the owner to the wheel. Looks like once that bond is broken, the wheel will turn to gold."

"So, I'm just supposed to waltz into the tower, sing a little tune, snip the cord, and everything will be back to normal?" Eleanor asked, chuckling at how ridiculous the whole plan sounded.

"Well, I can't give you all the answers. Just know that not everything is as it seems. Sometimes you have to look closer." Claire stood up and blew the torches out. "I really do think you should rest now. Goodnight."

Eleanor's mind was racing with what Claire had said.

"Why does everyone speak in riddles around here?" Eleanor said as she dropped the book back into the chest. She didn't even bother closing the lid. As she crawled back into bed, extreme exhaustion came upon her. As soon as she rested her head, she was asleep.

Eleanor dreamed, but the dreams weren't as they

normally were, which Eleanor chalked up to her taking on Lilura's role.

The dream was filled with shiny gold specks flying around, and images of Eleanor in her normal appearance quickly turned into the face of Lilura. The words from the riddles flooded her mind. In her dream, Lilura had been standing in the castle with the blade in her hand. The string was there, the one she needed to cut, but as soon as she tried to get close, R's crow came rushing at her, knocking the blade out of her hand and screaming in a language she had never heard before.

Eleanor sat straight up in bed and looked around. The room was still dark. She took a couple of deep breaths, calmed herself, and began to formulate a plan. Soon, a dreamless sleep came to her.

12

————

Eleanor woke with Fenek jumping at the foot of her bed. "Lilura, we must go!" She sat up slowly, outstretching her arms. She hadn't even noticed the scratchiness of the blanket as she slept.

"Alright, Fenek. Can we eat something first?"

"Yes, Claire has a vegetable spread in the dining area. You must eat quickly and gather supplies, and then we must go."

"I've got a plan—well, sort of."

"You'll need that," Claire said, entering the room. "I have also packed a sack of vegetables—oh, don't make that face. They're good for you."

"You sound like my mother," Eleanor said, rolling her eyes.

"Your mother is a very wise woman."

Eleanor ignored Claire's comment and took the satchel of vegetables.

"I'm just going to grab the things from the trunk and then I'll meet you for breakfast," she said.

Claire and Fenek left Eleanor alone in the room with the trunk, and Eleanor waited for a few moments before carefully taking the contents of the trunk: the book of riddles, blade, and empty bottles. She set them aside and then turned the satchel upside down, dumping all of the gross vegetables into the trunk.

She closed the lid, latched it, and placed the useful items into the satchel. For a second, she felt bad for the next person who came to Claire for help. Instead of discovering anything actually helpful, they'd end up with a bunch of rotten onions.

As she walked out the door, the torches blew themselves out, leaving the room Eleanor had called a sanctuary for a night completely dark. She met up with Fenek and set the satchel down by her feet under the table, hoping nobody would notice how light it was.

"Thanks for the vegetables," she told Claire. "I'm sure they will come in handy."

"They'll stop you from starving."

Eleanor looked at the spread on the table. Besides sautéed beets and onions, there was a huge pile of potatoes, something Eleanor could appreciate. She scooped them onto her plate, poured herself a glass of a very strange orange juice, and started shoveling food into her mouth. She hadn't realized how hungry she was until the warm potatoes hit her taste buds.

Eleanor took a drink of her juice and quickly gulped it down, ending with a "Yuck."

"It's carrot juice," Fenek said excitedly. "She makes the best around." He poured himself another glass.

"You can have mine," she said, pushing her almost-full glass toward her rabbit friend. She finished her potatoes, and Claire sent them on their way.

"I'm thinking we have several hours, but we will have to make our way through the town unseen, so we should probably head there now," Eleanor said.

"What is your plan?" Fenek asked.

"Well, we'll need to find some golden thread, cut it, and hope for the best."

"The real Lilura would have done better," Fenek said, frustrated.

Eleanor remembered what Claire had told her. Fenek's distant relative had been the one to temporarily destroy the wheel last time, so this mission to lead her wasn't coincidence.

"I'm sorry, Fenek. Last night, Claire told me how it was done before, by a rabbit."

Fenek looked up at her. "Yes. My great-great-grandpa. But the rest of the story was lost. I don't know how he did it, or I would have done it myself." Tears filled his eyes.

Eleanor bent down and wiped his eyes with her sleeve. "But I do."

"You do?" he asked, looking up at her.

"Sure do. But I'm going to need your help. Your name is going down in history for this, not mine," she said.

Fenek led her down the winding corridors and watched the sky carefully. He saw a large shadow coming over a building and pulled her into a dark corner.

"His crow is doing rounds," Fenek said. "We should wait here. Then we'll head to the stables."

"Stables?" Eleanor asked.

"Yes. They were abandoned long ago, once the king left. The townspeople let the horses roam free. There are no enslaved animals in this kingdom anymore. The horses come and help because they wish to, not because they are being held. There is a secret corridor hidden in the stables that leads directly to the dungeons."

Eleanor shuddered at the thought of going through the dungeons. In all of the fairytale books she had ever read, the dungeons were the most disgusting and cruel places to be.

"But you were saying that you know how the wheel was stopped before?" Fenek asked.

"Yes, Claire told me—"

"CLAIRE KNEW?" Fenek shouted. This was the first time Eleanor heard him speak so loudly.

"Shh. Yes, she told me last night."

"I went to her before the fairy fountain. I asked for help. She said she could not."

"Maybe she already knew the ridd—I mean prophecy. Maybe she knew you needed someone to help."

Fenek was still very much upset, but he sat down, waiting for Eleanor to explain.

"Anyway, there is a golden thread that connects the

owner to the wheel. It was cut last time, and the wheel turned to gold once the rabbit cut it."

"How did he see to cut it?"

"No clue. Maybe he tripped over it," Eleanor joked, which led to Fenek's mood getting even grumpier.

Fenek hopped out of the corner to check the skies, taking time to be away from Eleanor.

Eleanor quickly realized her joke had upset Fenek. She ducked out of the dark corner too and crept behind him. "I'm sorry again," she said. "Sometimes, I make jokes when I'm nervous."

"It's fine," he said sternly. "The skies are clear. We should go. Grab your bag and follow me."

Eleanor wrapped the bag around her shoulder and tried to keep up with Fenek. He was moving very quickly now, and Eleanor knew he was angry. They ran though abandoned buildings, shops that looked like they were perfectly preserved. Everything had been turned to gold—even the apples in the baskets outside the market. Nobody was to be seen, and Eleanor guessed they were either in hiding, had escaped to another portal, or were sleeping soundly in the Bird's Nest Café.

"How long ago did this happen?" she asked, completely out of breath.

"It has been five days. I think," he said, beginning to get confused.

"Fenek, are you okay?" Eleanor finally caught up to him. And that's when she noticed it. He was sitting next to a pile of golden flour sacks, and his ears and the top of his head started to turn to gold again. He tried to shake it off, but like last time, only specks of glitter fell. He was turning gold faster this time, and Eleanor guessed it was because they were getting closer to the wheel.

"Hold on, buddy," she said, rummaging through her pouch. She pulled out the vial that said *Fenek* and sprinkled some on him. "Here, you hold onto this. Just in case we get separated. You only need a few drops." She untied a bracelet from her wrist, looped it around the vial, and tied it around his neck.

His ears and head had turned back immediately, and he let out a sigh of relief. "I just need to rest a minute."

Eleanor took the time to look around the market. She knocked on a pile of peanuts and a loud *clang* rang out. She couldn't imagine how much this gold would be worth back home. She ran her fingers over the countertops and turned her hand to see fine specks of gold glitter had coated her skin.

She immediately brushed her hands onto her pants and hoped she wouldn't need to use her vial yet. Then, remembering the empty vials in the satchel, she figured she'd add them to her pouch with the others, just in case she found something to pour into them. She looked closely again at the empty vials and swore she saw something moving inside. She figured it was just the reflection off of the gold in the room and dropped them into her pouch. She pulled the blade out and secured it to her pants. The book folded up enough to fit into her front pocket. She looked into the bag to make sure it was empty and then told Fenek to hop in.

"How will I fit? It will be too heavy with me and the vegetables."

"Oh, I left those behind," Eleanor said. "Now hop in."

"You did what? Now we will starve! She is the only one in the city who has edible food. The rest is gold."

"Or poisoned," she said, quickly regretting dumping the vegetables into the trunk. Especially because they weren't just for her to eat, but for Fenek too. "I'm sorry. I just didn't want to lug around all that weight. Plus, there has to be other food. What are R and his goons eating?"

"Good point," he said, hopping into the bag.

"Maybe this will help conceal you so that you don't turn. I'm not sure how powerful the magic is. I'll need you to lead me to the stables."

13

Fenek kept his ears back and only poked his head out enough to give directions, but it was hard for him to really see, so they ended up going around in circles. Eleanor ducked down behind a huge post and set the bag down.

"This isn't working like I had hoped," she said. She sat and thought for a second before pulling out the blade from its sheath. She unwrapped it, revealing a shining red blade; it looked just like the ruby necklace her mother kept safe. Eleanor had only seen her wear it a couple of times, because her mother always said it was too fancy to wear while doing chores.

Fenek hopped out of the bag, and Eleanor and touched the tip of the blade to the material. A hole burned through. She retracted the blade and admired the handiwork. She looked at Fenek and used her thumb to measure the distance between his eyes. She placed her thumb at the first hole and then touched the blade at the measured distance. Another hole was burned through, and Eleanor wrapped the blade back up and dropped it into her pouch.

"Okay, now hop in," she said.

Fenek hopped in and peeked through the holes. "Oh, this is perfect!" he said. "I can see everything."

"Okay, let's hit the stables."

This time, they didn't run around in circles, and Fenek was able to lead her directly to the abandoned stables. It hadn't dawned on them that stables were filled with hay and wheat. They pushed open a door and had to look away. The sunlight that had streamed through the holes in the roof made the gold bales impossible to look at. Eleanor popped her sunglasses on and looked around. The place had clearly been abandoned for a long time, like Fenek had said. The whole building was in total disrepair. Holes filled the roof and the boards were separating, allowing sunlight to peek through everywhere.

"Where is the door?" she asked Fenek.

He hopped around, trying to remember where the entrance was. "I will have to find it again. It has been many years."

Eleanor helped him by looking closely at each of the walls. The golden bales were too hard to move, so she hoped the door wasn't hidden behind one.

"Over here. I have found it!" Fenek said.

Eleanor looked at the tiny hole in the wall. "Fenek, you expect me to fit into that door?"

"Oh, if you can make it into my home, you can make it here. It was the rabbits who made this passage. You may just have to *think small*."

"Here we go again," Eleanor said under her breath. At first, she laughed at the idea of *thinking small*, but then she remembered that she was in a fairytale book, and maybe that was quite possible. This must be part of her ability to change appearance on a whim. She also wondered if there was a way to enter any door in this kingdom without doing something outrageous.

Fenek disappeared into the hole, and Eleanor could hear him calling for her to come through. She told herself to be small and attempted to squeeze through the entrance. She made it halfway through before forgetting to keep *thinking small*.

"Fenek," she said. "I'm stuck."

"*Think small.*"

She told herself, again, to be small, and she slid right through.

"Huh, it worked," she said, brushing the dust and dirt off of her clothes.

"Of course it worked. You're an enchantress. You can make yourself big or small."

"I'll have to remember that," Eleanor said.

"Please do."

"Oh, hush. Just lead us to the dungeons."

Eleanor slid her sunglasses up on the top of her head and checked her surroundings. It seemed as though they were inside a wall. She could see all of the support beams and mouse nests.

"If you make me squeeze though another hole, I'm not going to be happy."

"Oh, no, there's a hidden door this time," he said proudly. "It's behind a painting."

"Did a rabbit do that too?"

"Oh yes," he said with a smirk. He pressed his nose against a small crack in the wall and Eleanor heard a soft *click*.

The wall opened a bit and Eleanor pushed it open. The entrance opened up to an odd room. Eleanor looked at the walls and could see that they were made of a slimy brick. A fireplace that held no fire was across the room, and Eleanor could barely make out the furniture covered in sheets.

"I thought we were in the dungeons. Why would there be a giant painting, a fireplace, and a couch down here?" she asked.

"This was the dungeon master's study," Fenek said. He hopped over to a desk that Eleanor barely saw. She remembered that rabbits had better vision in the dark than she had. He brought her a pack of matches. "Can you light a torch?"

She found a torch on the wall next to her, and it immediately caught fire when she held the match near it. Just the one torch illuminated the entire place and Eleanor found it to be a cozy little area, especially down in the dungeons.

"Are you sure it is safe for us to be here?" she asked, uncovering the couch.

"Yes. This is why we came this way. R is most likely up in the king's chambers with the wheel. The wizard's tower is right off of the chambers, which is where I imagine his crow is perched. The dungeons are of no use to him."

Eleanor remembered her conversation with Claire about the thread linking R to the wheel. He probably couldn't even leave the chambers. It reassured Eleanor a little to know that they were most likely safe here. At least for a while.

Eleanor's stomach grumbled and the regret of leaving the food behind returned. It was as though Fenek read her mind though, because he began rummaging through desk drawers and pulled out some salted pork. He looked at her with eyebrows raised and joined her on the couch.

"How old is that stuff?"

"Probably a decade or so. But it's salted and cured and only gets better as it ages."

"I didn't know rabbits ate meat."

"We don't. I've heard that though." He handed the package to Eleanor, who studied it apprehensively.

"What will you eat?"

"Don't worry. I ate enough this morning to cover me until much later."

Eleanor tore off a small piece and sniffed it. Fenek let out a small snort and giggle. She tasted it and to her surprise, Fenek was right. She munched on it a little and wished she could light the fireplace. She also knew that time seemed to move more quickly in this realm, and she didn't want to lose track of time. She dropped the salted pork into her pouch and pulled out the book.

She had folded the corner of the page Claire had showed her so she could quickly reference it anytime.

She read the riddle closely, making sure Claire had given her proper information. Eleanor wasn't sure who could be trusted here, especially since she had already been given a sleeping draught, and Claire had denied Fenek help in the first place. It was like she had said:

While the kingdom slumbers in beds of gold,
and the moon hangs high and the night grows cold,
the day without curse will begin anew,
when the rabbit burns the thread in two.

Eleanor pulled the blade from its sheath and looked it over. Its bright-red glow was a curiosity to Eleanor. She pressed her thumb against its sharp edge, half-expecting it to cut her. It didn't, but it did leave a burn. She pulled her hand back quickly and studied her thumb. The burn had scarred and faded as quickly as it had appeared. She touched the tip of the blade with her finger, expecting to feel a prick, but again, it burned at the touch. She released her finger, but it had already healed. She figured it was probably part of her powers as a sorceress in training.

"When the rabbit burns the thread in two," she said aloud. She opened her pouch and looked inside. The contents that filled the chest back at Claire's must have belonged to the rabbit. The ruby blade was the one the riddle was talking about. He must have used what was once in the empty vials to help him too; Eleanor just didn't know how.

Fenek, not paying attention to Eleanor, creaked the main door to the study open and peered outside.

She looked around and studied the room a bit more. Paintings of men and women in chainmail, scholars, and the king covered the walls. She looked at their outfits and remembered a part of the prophecy she hadn't figured out: the disguise. There had been nothing to help disguise herself in that chest, and nothing in the pouch. She was left only with a potion that would stop her from turning to gold and a couple empty vials. She had hoped that maybe she would find something, but the time was fading, and she still had nothing.

Fenek saw the disappointment on her face.

"What part is troubling you?" he asked.

"I don't have a disguise."

14

Fenek shook his head, leaving little sparks of gold flying into the air and settling with the dust.

"You have a built-in disguise. Lilura—I mean Eleanor—you can change your appearance at will, remember?"

"Yes, but I don't know how."

Eleanor looked at the clock and saw that it was nearly eleven o'clock at night already. Time definitely moved faster here. She packed up her things and followed Fenek out the door. It was nearly impossible to see anything, so Eleanor stretched out her hands, feeling for the wall. Her hands immediately soaked up the slime that had settled on the brick.

"Yuck!" she yelled, forgetting the need to be quiet. Her voice echoed down the empty corridor and she heard a soft "shush" behind her. "Sorry," she whispered.

"It's fine, until we get around this corner. We will be cutting through the kitchens," he said.

"Won't we be seen?"

"Not likely. Do not forget that this does not operate as a functioning palace anymore. The king and his servants are long gone. R is just held up here because he is familiar with it. There is a back staircase that will lead to the main chambers. From there is a secret entrance that leads to the king's chambers."

"How do you know all of this?" Eleanor said, forgetting everything he had just told her.

"I lived here as a young rabbit. When the king was in power, rabbits were used as gardeners. Nobody can pull vegetables out of the garden quite like a rabbit," he said. "I was too young to garden, but my parents and grand-parents did. My siblings and I played around the palace, discovering and creating all of the secret passages."

Eleanor wanted to hear so much more about the kingdom and Fenek's days in the palace, but she knew there was no time. According to Claire, sunrise happened directly after midnight, and it was almost time.

As they rounded the corner, Eleanor could see light. She was happy that it wasn't like the light reflecting off of the gold.

"Why hasn't the palace turned to gold?" Eleanor asked in a whisper.

"An enchantment of some sort, I'm sure. The king may have put a protection on the castle from the last time the wheel was used."

Fenek grabbed a carrot on his way through the kitchen and led Eleanor to the back staircase. Unlike the dungeons, the staircase wasn't completely blacked out, and to Eleanor's relief, the walls weren't slimy. They carefully climbed the stairs, pausing every now and then to listen. When they heard nothing, they continued. Eleanor had never seen so many stairs before, especially ones that wrapped around and around. After what seemed like a million stairs, Eleanor stopped and leaned against the wall, breathing heavily. Fenek was half a staircase up when he realized that Eleanor wasn't behind him. He motioned for her to come, so she took another second to catch her breath and caught up to him.

The last of the stairs came into Eleanor's view and she stood in awe of what awaited her at the top.

15

The entire room was marble, and the ceiling went on for ages. She immediately wondered about the lives of the people who lived in these chambers when the kingdom was still under the king's control. She pictured princesses and the royals dancing among the marble halls. She was lost in her imagination when she heard a voice that was not Fenek's.

She ducked out of the way and watched Fenek hide as well. Two short dwarf-like creatures went walking by, speaking in a language Eleanor couldn't understand. Once they had passed, Eleanor waited, listening carefully for more. When no voices could be heard, she snuck over by Fenek.

"Who are they?" she asked.

"Not sure. I've never seen creatures like them before. R probably brought them along from another realm."

"So, what are we going to do about them?" she asked.

"Maybe a diversion will help. Use your song."

"But we don't know where they are going. Plus, I need my voice to be a surprise. What if R hears it and knows I'm coming?"

"Oh, dear. I think you are right. But I do have an idea. That blade of yours. It burned through that fabric on the bag. Do you think if you held it up against something long enough, it would start a fire?"

"Maybe," Eleanor said, unsure of where Fenek's idea was going.

"Okay, good. Let's go further in. When I tell you to, I want you to set all of the drapes in the next room on fire. And then you'll run until you see a large painting with a knight on it. You'll see that his left knee panel opens. *Think small.*"

"Wait, what? You want me to set fire to what?"

"The drapes. We need a diversion, and unless you have something better, this is your choice."

"But we can't just destroy such a beautiful place!" Eleanor whispered sternly. She knew what the cost of fabric was back home and knew her mother could only dream of having such beautiful fabric to make curtains with.

"It will be destroyed anyway. It is no use to the villagers. Now, I must go. I will meet you at our meeting place."

"Wait—where will you be?"

"Oh, rabbits do not like fire. I will be through the knee panel. Remember, *think small.*"

"Right," Eleanor said sarcastically. She followed Fenek into another jaw-dropping room. This one had a huge four-poster bed with elegant drapes all around it. Lavish mirrors covered the gold-and-purple wallpaper. Eleanor had only dreamed of a bedroom like this. She felt guilty for a moment when she realized that she would have to set the whole room on fire. Fenek had said that the palace was of no use, but Eleanor remembered how important history was. Last time, she was told off for setting things on fire, and now she was being asked to.

She knew Fenek was right though. She didn't have any other ideas, and time was running out. She opened the far window so that the smoke would waft up to the tower and alert the crow.

"Okay, go!" Fenek said, hopping through the far door and out of sight.

Eleanor pulled the blade out and set it against the first set of draperies. She made sure to press the unsharpened side to the curtain, so that it would not cut the fabric before the fire could catch. Once the first set was ablaze, she went to each windowpane until the whole room filled with smoke. She quickly ran out of the room, coughing, and searched the hallway for the portrait Fenek was talking about. She saw nothing.

Eleanor heard shouting in a foreign language and heavy boots coming her way. The smoke must have reached the tower. She kept searching for the portrait, but her eyes were stained with tears from the smoke. She saw a large marble statue and ducked behind that as the dwarves she saw before went running past her.

She waited a second and took off, hoping to find Fenek.

She heard a "psst" and turned around to see the painting with a hole right above the knight's knee. Relief came over her until she realized she was too big.

"*Think small,*" Fenek's voice rang through her mind. She thought of herself as small as a mouse and squeezed through the hole. Once again, Fenek had led her to another secret hideout. Like the passage at the stables, this one led behind the walls as well.

"It worked!" Fenek said. "But we must go. It won't take them very long to put the fire out."

Remembering what the room looked like when Eleanor had left, she knew Fenek had misjudged the size of the fire he had asked her to start.

"But what if there are more?"

"Oh, no. There will not be more. The imp is nothing but a wizard, and wizards think they are invincible. He wouldn't think he needed more protection than that. He's alone." Fenek started down the secret passage that mirrored the main hallway.

"Does he have more crows?" she asked.

"No, that would be murderous," he said. "But his crow is linked to him, though I am not sure how." Eleanor sighed with relief that she only had to keep watch for one crow.

Soon, they came to the end of the wall and Eleanor saw another hole cutout. Fenek peeked out and made sure all was clear. Once he was sure, he whispered to Eleanor to follow him as he hopped out of the hole.

She could hear a shrill voice.

"Turn, turn, turn. All will be gold."

She turned to look at Fenek and realized that his ears were turning again. She caught his attention and pointed to his ears. Fenek sprinkled some of his potion on and then snuck into the king's room. Eleanor tried to stop him, but it was too late. She knew that if she crawled out of the painting, she would be seen for sure. *Thinking small* only seemed to help momentarily so that she could fit into tight spaces. So instead, she peeked out and did a sweep of the room.

That's when she saw the clock. It was two minutes to twelve. The second part of the prophecy was about to pass. Eleanor only had minutes.

She continued to scan the room—and then she saw him and his wheel.

16

R was standing not more than a foot from the spinning wheel. Eleanor remembered her conversation with Claire and knew he had to stay close because of the thread connecting them. Next to the wheel was a stack of wheat. R would throw wheat into the wheel and it would magically disappear. Something told Eleanor that this was how he was turning the city into gold. She looked around and saw Fenek, or what used to be her rabbit friend. He was crouched under an ornate table, but instead of panicking like she imagined he would, Eleanor saw something that made her want to scream. Fenek was completely gold. One paw was wrapped around his vial, but the wheel had worked too quickly. Eleanor's heart sank. She had no help and only minutes to turn the wheel to gold and defeat R.

The crow's call stunned Eleanor. He had made it back after doing his round of the city. R turned toward the window and began conversing to the bird in the same language Eleanor had heard before. This was her chance, as he wasn't paying attention to the wheel.

At first, she thought about saving Fenek, but then she remembered the queen's warning in the last story she was in. If she didn't save the kingdom, Fenek would never make it back. He had enough in his vial for her to turn him back once all of this was over.

"Maybe he's safer this way anyway," she said to herself.

Eleanor looked into her pouch again and hoped new supplies had magically appeared. She thought of the best disguise she could, but nothing about her had changed. Her plan was already falling apart.

She squinted and looked closely to see if she could spot the thread, but she couldn't. She knew she would have to get closer. Watching the crow carefully, she snuck out of the painting and into the room, hoping it wouldn't give her away. Luckily, he was too focused on speaking to R. She pulled the blade back out to have it ready to snip the line, but even as she got closer, she couldn't see it.

Claire was wrong. There wasn't a thread connecting them. Just then, something that Eleanor hadn't been warned about, nor prepared for, happened. The blade let out a high-pitched squeal as she brought it close to the wheel. R immediately turned around.

But instead of a surprised look on his face, a sinister grin appeared. He reached in his pocket and pulled out two pieces of cotton.

Before Eleanor could start her song, or even say anything, R shoved the cotton into his ears.

"It won't work, girl," he said. "But where is your friend? Perhaps he'd now make a lovely doorstop."

Brutus, Eleanor thought. He had warned R of their plan.

"The enchantress of old sent me," Eleanor said, mustering up all of the bravery she could find. The words came out in a shout though instead of anything beautiful. Eleanor hadn't been concentrating enough.

He laughed maniacally and pointed to his ears. He couldn't hear a thing. Eleanor's eyes welled up with tears. She had failed.

R's laughter stopped abruptly. He gave Eleanor a puzzled look.

Just as confused as he seemed to be, Eleanor looked down at her legs and saw that her body was flashing between Eleanor of America and the enchantress. This was not good. Eleanor wondered if this was what would happen if she failed a quest as a character in the book. Would she be stuck there forever as her real self? Eleanor started to panic.

"No, there is still time," she said to herself. "The clock hasn't struck yet."

She shook the thoughts from her mind and brought her attention back to the wheel.

Eleanor started waving the blade around where the thread should be, hoping that it would catch it and cut something. With no luck, she stood frozen.

R started to spin the wheel again and began to chant. Eleanor knew she had to get out of there. She knew Fenek's advice would be to create a diversion, but her voice was powerless, so she threw a stone she found on a table toward the far end of the room. As soon as R looked away, she darted through the painting, hoping nobody had seen her.

He quickly looked back to find the room empty.

"FIND HER!" he ordered the crow.

Eleanor leaned against the wall, defeated. The clock struck twelve.

17

The sun will rise twice, and the imp will concede.
To destroy the wheel, you must take on a disguise.
Turn the wheel into gold before the sun will rise.

She remembered what Claire had said about the sun rising shortly after midnight. There was no way she could do this.

Her appearance flashed again. Eleanor curled up in a ball and started to sob. She would never make it home, never see her mother again. And Fenek, poor Fenek! He had been turned to gold and it was all her fault. Claire had been right all along; magical books were not something to toy with.

Claire! Claire's words rushed into her mind. *Just know that not everything is as it seems. Sometimes you have to look closer.*

Eleanor sprang up and willed herself to be brave

and try again. She dumped the contents of her pouch out of her bag and onto the floor.

"How am I supposed to see an invisible thread?" she whispered to herself.

The vials! Eleanor grabbed the empty vials and peered into one.

"Look closer," she said.

She figured that if she could think herself to be small enough to fit through a rabbit hole, she might be able to see through an empty vial. Suddenly she saw the sparkle that she had seen before. The vials weren't empty; the liquid inside was barely visible. Eleanor knew what she had to do, but hoped she could do it quickly enough, and before the guards came back.

She crawled out of the hole in the wall again and ran straight toward R and the wheel, dumping the contents of the not-so-empty vial into the air. The thread connecting the two appeared in gold, and Eleanor reached for her blade.

R began chanting faster, and Eleanor felt herself turning to gold. She grabbed her the vial labeled *Lilura* and took a big swig, hoping it would stop her from turning while she did this. She let the red leather fall to the floor, brought the blade up by the hilt, and swung it down onto the thread.

Because the thread was made of pure gold, it fought the blade, but eventually, Eleanor broke through and the thread fell to the ground in two pieces.

"NOO!" R shouted, as he watched the wheel turn into pure gold. It stopped spinning and just sat sparkling under the light of the rising sun.

"You will pay!" he shouted, trying to turn the wheel back. He moved his hands on it, trying to manually move it, while chanting the same words as before.

"Actually, according to a prophecy I heard, it's your turn to pay," Eleanor said, wiping the tears from her eyes.

As the words left her mouth, R's color started to fade and in a matter of minutes, he was, as he had put it, a perfect doorstop.

Eleanor ran to Fenek, popped the stopper on his vial and poured it over his head. At first, nothing happened, and Eleanor's heart began to race. "It can't be too late. I did it! I saved the kingdom!" Eleanor shouted. "There *has* to be a happily ever after."

What she thought had been a weird reflection or shadow, was actually a small twitch in Fenek's ears. His ears were twitching. The gold was fading.

"Oh, Fenek!" she said while hugging the half-golden rabbit.

"Did we do it?" he asked, trying to break free of both the spell and her hug.

"Yes! We did it, Fenek!"

18

Eleanor and Fenek climbed up into the wizard tower and looked over the city. The sun was rising, but instead of the city shining under the new morning sun, there was a soft yellow glow. Everything was returning to the natural order.

Eleanor looked at the beauty of the city and wished she had a chance to explore. But she also knew how this worked. She and Fenek would make their way back to Claire one last time, and then Eleanor would appear back in her room.

"How did you do it?" Fenek asked, as he and Eleanor made their way out the main doors of the palace.

"I guess you could say things can be different than they appear."

"Now who's speaking in riddles?" Fenek teased.

"Oh, look at you, making jokes!"

Fenek shook his head and smiled. "You could stay, you know. Stop by the fountain and get another prophecy. You may be sent to another realm, but you're good at this."

"Oh, Fenek. No, I belong at home. This is Lilura's job."

Fenek's head dropped.

"But we'll remember this adventure!" she said, patting him on the head. She hoped her words brought him comfort, even if she wasn't sure what she had said was true.

Now that it was daylight, and the fate of the city didn't rely on Eleanor saving everyone, she and Fenek were able to walk slowly back to Claire's cellar, as Eleanor called it.

Townspeople began coming out of hiding and lining the streets, clapping for the pair of heroes. Eleanor stopped in front of the fountain fairy and stood up on the bench.

"Can I have your attention please!" she shouted.

Fenek hopped around nervously. "What are you doing? If you speak too much, they will know!" he said.

"It doesn't matter. I'll be leaving soon," she whispered to her friend. "If I may have your attention," she shouted again. "I'd like to take a second to recognize a very brave rabbit! A rabbit who has saved this city— your city, just as his great-great-grand-rabbit before him. He is your hero. I helped him along, but he saved everyone."

The clapping and cheers grew louder. Eleanor bent down and picked Fenek up. The cheers continued.

Fenek looked up at Eleanor and just shook his head. Tiny flecks of gold glitter flew into the wind.

"Let's go return these supplies to Claire," she said.

As they continued down the streets, more and more villagers came out and joined the celebration. It didn't take long for Eleanor's announcement to make its way through the city. Soon, everyone was shouting Fenek's name.

Before opening the door to Claire's house, Fenek stopped Eleanor.

"You didn't have to do that. I was a hunk of metal while you saved the day," he said.

"I wouldn't have been able to do any of it if you hadn't found me on that hill, or if you hadn't shown me the secret passageways and to *think small.* He almost turned me into gold, but I was able to disappear back into the hole in the painting. It's all because of you. I just carried out the plan." She patted him on the head again and opened the door.

The scent of onions wafted out of the door once more, but this time Eleanor was happy to breathe in that disgusting smell. She and Fenek hurried happily into the main room, where Claire was sitting. She was writing in something.

"We did it, we did it!" Fenek shouted happily.

"I see that. I will need you to tell me the whole story, riddle keeper," she said, looking directly at Fenek.

He looked at Eleanor and she winked back. She had spent the rest of the walk back to Claire's home filling him in on what he had missed, so that he could answer questions whenever he was asked how he saved the city.

"And you, girl, what does one do with a *book* once it is written?"

"We keep them on shelves so we can go back to them any chance we get," Eleanor said, smiling.

"And do you return often to the books you read?" Claire asked.

"Sometimes, but I'm not sure I'd ever reread some of them. Some stories just stay with you forever and you never forget even the smallest detail," she said, looking at Fenek.

"What will happen when the real Lilura returns with a prophecy already fulfilled?" Fenek asked Claire.

"It's never happened before. But I need a helper here. If you could talk Lilura into coming to me, she will never look for a silly riddle to solve again."

As Fenek and Claire continued their conversation, Eleanor found the chest full of vegetables and laughed. She placed the blade and the other contents of her pouch into the chest. She reached into her pocket and felt another something soft. A piece of wheat. She took a look at it, then let it drop back into her pocket. She thought that just maybe, the token would make it home as the purple leaf had.

She returned to her friends and was about to tell them goodbye, when Claire asked if she could stick around for a feast. Celebratory feasts were common in the last chapters of fairytales, so Eleanor agreed.

She, Fenek, and Claire sat for hours, laughing and pushing onion pieces around on their plates. Soon, they were all sleepy, and Eleanor knew it was time. Fenek was already sound asleep, head down on the table with his ears in the turnip puree. Eleanor kissed his head and turned to Claire.

"Thank you for all of your help. Your clue was what saved everyone."

"I like a good riddle every now and then," she said with a wink. "Have a safe journey back to your realm. If you ever happen to find yourself in our kingdom again, you have a bed waiting for you."

She opened her door and sent Eleanor on her way. She walked through the city and finally reached the fields of wheat. This time, she was confident that she could run through them with arms stretched out. She felt the softness on her fingertips. She was about to hit the top of the hill when she vanished.

19

Eleanor landed on her bed with the book on her lap. A rough sketch of an enchantress and a rabbit asleep at a giant dinner table sat right above the words *The End*. She was back in her normal clothes, but she patted down her pockets, looking for whatever it was that crossed over with her. She felt something soft, reached into her pocket, and pulled out a strand of wheat. She twirled it carefully for a moment, remembering Fenek and his sweet, yet sometimes annoying, nervousness, before tucking it away in a box of hidden treasures. The leaf from Nightshade Forest was resting on her bed, and she added that to her collection as well.

Next to the leaf was the fairytale book she had checked out from the library. Eleanor chuckled at the coincidence that she had held the answers to what had happened in her hands a few hours prior to vanishing. She wished she hadn't browsed through the Rumpelstiltskin story so fast earlier that day.

She reached over and grabbed a pen. She scribbled "Rumpelstiltskin" under the chapter title in her book, just in case anyone else managed to get trapped in the City of Gold.

For a while, Eleanor just sat there, remembering everything that had happened in the book. In fact, she was still a little lost in her adventure in the golden city when she heard her mother coming. Eleanor closed her treasure box and tucked it under the corner of her feather mattress. She fluffed up the corner just as her mother appeared in the doorway.

"Eleanor dear, is everything alright?"

"Yes, Mama. Would it be alright if I went back to the library?"

"You were just there, dear, and I thought Mrs. O'Leary had closed early."

"Yes, but I really need to bring this one back," Eleanor said, looking at the Grimm book on her bed. "Maybe she hasn't left yet!"

"Well, alright. But wear an extra sweater under your—"

Eleanor rushed out the door before her mother could say "coat."

Blustery winds tried to take Eleanor's bag, but she was able to clutch it before it took off into the air. The storm had gotten much worse, and Eleanor knew they were looking at several feet of snow. Mrs. O'Leary always closed the day after a bad storm because she had to wait until the snow was removed from the steps and sidewalks.

In a half-walk, half-run, Eleanor made her way

back to the giant building. She was thrilled when she saw the lamps were still lit. Mrs. O'Leary wasn't gone yet. Eleanor's heart sank when she remembered the door had locked behind her earlier that day.

Eleanor had to get back into the library. She knew her book was acting strangely when she was there earlier, and she had to know why. She couldn't go into another story before understanding the book's magic.

She carefully climbed the stairs, leaving her footprints behind. The doors wouldn't budge. Eleanor sank down in the snow, ignoring the dampness seeping through her pants.

"I guess I'll have to wait," she said to herself. The magical book thumped in her bag. "Yeah, I know. There's something special about this place," she said, looking at her bag.

Then Eleanor remembered something. Mrs. O'Leary always used the side entrance to leave once she locked the big doors. The lanterns were still lit, so she was definitely still there. Eleanor imagined she was just getting everything in order before heading out. One thing Mrs. O'Leary hated was messy bookshelves.

Eleanor brushed the snow off of her butt and headed to the side of the library. She found a small door with mounds of snow piled in front of it. Eleanor said a little prayer and tried the knob. A smile crept over her face as she heard the *click* of the door opening.

20

"Mrs. O'Leary?" she said in a hushed tone. It was still a library, after all. When no response came, Eleanor pushed her whole body through the door and shut it tightly so the wind couldn't grab it.

Eleanor wiggled her shoes, letting the fluffy flakes fall off her boots. Luckily, the snow so far was just the light stuff that didn't stick to everything. These were the sort of flakes Eleanor liked to catch on her tongue. But she didn't have time to play in the snow. She needed answers about this fairytale book, and why it seemed to come alive when she was in or near the library.

Dusty books of all sorts formed stacks to the ceiling. She had never been in this portion of the building before, and Eleanor wondered if these were books nobody wanted to read, or if they were ones that Mrs. O'Leary had yet to put out.

Eleanor blew off some of the books and a huge

cloud of dust filled the air, causing her to cough. She swatted at the particles clouding her vision until the room cleared. She looked around, half-expecting Mrs. O'Leary to come charging in to see who was breaking into her library. When she didn't hear the *click-clack* of shoes, she looked at the books she blew off. They looked like books her dad would read in front of his woodstove while taking long puffs from his cobb pipe.

She thought about asking Mrs. O'Leary if she could borrow one for him, but her thoughts were interrupted once again by her book moving in her satchel. This time, instead of hiding it, she pulled the book from her bag and held it tightly in her hands. Maybe it would lead her to the answers.

"Okay, you're in charge," she whispered to the book.

Either her eyes were still messed up from the blinding gold, or what she was seeing was real, because the *f* on the book began to glow upon her words.

Eleanor found herself tiptoeing toward the lobby, but she told herself that she wasn't exactly sneaking around; she was just paying a visit to Mrs. O'Leary.

Eleanor found a few steps and a door with a frosted glass window. The letters were backwards, but she was sure it said "EXIT."

Carefully, she turned the knob and pushed the door open. It led straight to the lobby. Eleanor looked to see if Mrs. O'Leary was behind the circulation desk, but once again her chair was empty. She did a quick scan and saw the door to the room she had crashed in earlier was open.

She could hear Mrs. O'Leary humming. The book started to pull Eleanor in that direction. Before Eleanor could decide if she wanted to spy on the librarian, or turn around and run back home, the book had her at the door.

Eleanor took a deep breath and peeked into the room. Mrs. O'Leary was facing the back wall, but it wasn't the old lady that she was looking at: the books in the room were glowing. Eleanor squinted and saw a flutter behind her librarian: wings.

Eleanor stared, not paying attention to the book. It almost flew out of her hands toward the secret room. She lurched forward, securing the book firmly in her grasp.

A sigh of relief escaped her mouth, and she covered her mouth and ducked out of sight, just as Mrs. O'Leary spun around.

"Hello? Who's there?"

Her wings began to glow.

"Ah, we have another book in our midst, now don't we?" she said, carefully closing the door behind her. As soon as Mrs. O'Leary walked through the threshold, she turned back into the lady with a messy bun and cat-eye glasses.

Eleanor ran as fast as she could out of the main lobby and back through the side entrance. Once she felt the cold rush of the icy air fill her lungs, she knew she was safe.

"Mrs. O'Leary? A fairy?" she said, breathless.

Her mind buzzed, trying to piece together everything she saw. She looked down at the book in her hands, which had gone limp once outside.

"There are other books like you?" she asked in a whisper.

Carefully, she dropped the book into her bag and started home. Mrs. O'Leary had the answers she needed, but she didn't know if she wanted to give the book up just yet. It was a special gift from her father— a rare Christmas gift.

Eleanor's stomach knotted. She knew it belonged to the library with Mrs. O'Leary—or whoever she really was—but there were more stories to disappear into, more kingdoms to save.

"Maybe just one more, and then I'll return it." Eleanor walked past the front doors of the library, not noticing Mrs. O'Leary peering out the glass window.

"I'll just have to keep you away from the library for a little while longer, so Mrs. O'Leary doesn't suspect anything," she told the book, giving her bag a good pat.

Behind her, the library became dark.

21

Eleanor's father came home early that night with news that he would have a few days off due to the weather.

"Maybe we can get some reading in, hey?" he asked Eleanor, scooping her into a hug. "Why don't I go change into some dry clothes and you grab that fairytale book of yours?"

"Oh," Eleanor said nervously. There was no way she was going to open that book until she had answers. The *City of Gold* had been too close; she had almost failed.

"What? Not a fan of it anymore?" her dad said, disappointed.

"Oh no! I love my book. It's just that I've been so involved in the stories today, my eyes are a little sore."

"Well, I could read, you know?"

"You haven't read *Alice* in a while."

"Alright. *Alice* it is. Meet me out here in five," he said with a wink.

Eleanor kept a tight grasp on her bag and held her breath until making it safely into her room. She pulled the book out and stared at it. The *f* had gone back to normal and it looked like a plain old book.

"You're going to get me into some trouble, you know," she said in an almost-stern voice.

Instead of placing the book carefully on its spot on her shelf, she forced it into her box of treasures and shoved it deep under her bed. Eleanor knew nobody could find that book until she knew everything about it.

Her head was still buzzing at what she had seen at the library. "A real fairy?" she whispered.

"Eleanor!"

"I'll be there in a second," she called back.

Eleanor grabbed her copy of *Alice's Adventures in Wonderland* and carefully shut her door behind her, leaving her crazy adventures locked away for now.

The END

Coming Soon:
The Cave of Stories
Book Three of Eleanor Mason's Literary Adventures

PROLOGUE

M rs. O'Leary twisted the key into the door and gave it a swift turn, pushing the grand wooden door open. She breathed in the smell of books and sighed.

On quiet mornings like this, the smell always brought her back to the first time she stepped through those doors as a child, and again twenty-five years later as the librarian.

She had only been there for two years when her first magical book arrived. A small toad-like man stood on his tippy-toes in front of the front desk. Mrs. O'Leary was busy writing out cards for the stack of new books to her right. She hadn't heard him come in.

"Ahem." The man cleared his throat and tried to stretch his body even more. "Excuse me."

"Hmm?" Mrs. O'Leary asked, looking around.

"Down here."

She peered over the desk to find the man, in a singed jacket and leather boots with the toe blown out. She had never seen such a creature before. She had only read of them in fairytales. She took off her glasses, rubbed them with her handkerchief, and put them back on, looking over the counter once again.

"Oh dear," she said. "How can I, uh, be of service to you?"

"I need to return this book," he said, handing it to her.

She carefully took the book from his hands and promptly dropped it. "Ick," she said, looking at the slime hanging from her fingers.

"Ah, yeah, sometimes that happens in the bogswamp."

"Bogswamp?" she said, looking for an appropriate place to wipe the green slime from her hand.

"You've heard of the bogswamp, I'm sure. It's where I'm from," he said, handing her the book back.

She grabbed it with one finger and a thumb and set it on her desk.

"No, I haven't. And this book does not belong here."

"But he gave me your card with this address."

"Who?"

"The wizard. He said before the book causes anymore trouble, I must return the book to you. That you can put it on its rightful shelf, and we would be safe from portal-hoppers."

Mrs. O'Leary stared at the book. She looked back at the man.

"May I see the card?" she asked.

He dug in his coat pocket and retrieved a crumpled square of paper about the size of a standard playing card.

Mrs. L. Saffron
Chief Librarian
Keeper of Magical Books

Mrs. O'Leary read it twice and stared at the word "magical" for a bit before turning her attention back to the man.

"I'm sorry. Mrs. Saffron was the previous librarian and she never told me anything about magical books. I'm afraid I can't be of service to you," she said, trying to return the book to him.

"No, ma'am. This is serious business. I can't bring this back home. It brings trouble. People portal hopping, bringing magic from faraway lands. Even—" he leaned in close, "—*mortals* are crossing over."

Mrs. O'Leary giggled at the word "mortals."

"But I was left with no instructions. And I am not a keeper of magical books. I am sorry." She placed the card on top of the book and returned it to the man.

He hung his head and started toward the door.

Mrs. O'Leary closed her eyes for a moment trying

to figure out if she had been daydreaming. Then, she heard soggy footsteps hurrying back her way.

"Mrs. O'Leary?" the man asked.

"Yes?" she asked, peering at the man even closer than before. She had specifically avoided telling him her name.

"You said you're not the keeper of magical books, but it says right here you are!" he said happily.

"No, that was Mrs. Saffron."

"Here, look!" He handed the card back to her.

She looked down and once again cleaned her glasses. But there, in shiny gold print was her name.

~~Mrs. Saffron~~
Mrs. A. O'Leary
Chief Librarian
Keeper of Magical Books

The previous name had been scratched off perfectly with the matching gold print. There was no way the little man from the bogswamp could have changed it. The card was magic.

"I'm not sure what all of this is about, but I still don't have a place for books in that—um—condition. She frowned at the damp book he was holding.

"Well, that's not my problem anymore, ma'am." He threw the book up onto the desk and disappeared with a *pop*.

Mrs. O'Leary stood in the stock room staring at the book on the top shelf with the ugly green stain. Her wings fluttered, but they had grown tired after all these years.

"One more to go, and my job here will be complete," she said.

ACKNOWLEDGMENTS

I honestly don't even know where to begin. This journey has been quite the whirlwind and I never thought I'd publish two books during a pandemic, but here I am.

First, I have to thank my husband, Mike. Way back before Eleanor's Literary Adventures became a thought, he was there, noticing the girl hiding behind her book in front of her locker before school started. Yep, seventeen years ago he saw the invisible me. And you know what? He's been rooting for me since. We are team, he and I and I wouldn't be sitting her typing on my awesome keyboard—which he also bought me —if it weren't for his *you can do it* attitude. Because honestly, most days I have a *this isn't remotely possible* attitude. So, thank you. Thank you for believing in me, believing in Eleanor and Fenek, and whatever other imaginary friends (I mean characters) I bring into our family.

Next, to my kiddos. Your love for books and stories

are the reason I'm doing this. I want you to know that through any pandemic, or really anything that the world throws at you, that you can achieve your dreams. It may not be the way you had thought it would happen, but it can still happen, if you believe. Thank you for being my alpha readers, and for loving on Elfie, Fenek, and Mrs. O'Leary. Thank you for listening to "mommy just has to write one more part and then I'll be up," so many times this past year. I love you both with all of my heart.

To Unc, for creating these maps that take me back to when I was a kid. I know the trees and the wheat are super annoying to draw, but yet you do it for me. I appreciate you and it means a lot to me that you're willing to spend hours and a ton of ink on these maps.

To my friends and family, thank you for asking about, purchasing, and hyping my books and believing in my dreams. Bookstagram family, this includes you. I never in a million years thought that I would have a group of people from all over the world excited about my stories, but there you are. I can't name all of you, but gosh you're an amazing group of people. Hina, Nichole, Darby, Sophie, Karley, Miranda, Cassie, Beck, and Chloe—thank you for the friendship, advice, and the chance to gush about books.

Hina, thank you for the gorgeous covers. And logo. And continuous support and friendship. I don't believe in coincidences and I know you and I became friends for a reason.

To my street team: Amanda, Estelle, Stephanie, Kelsey, and Mandy, you helped make this book a reality too and I am so glad to have you in on this epic adventure with me.

To the libraries that carry my books—thank you. Thank you for sharing this with the children in our community. You've helped make my dream a reality. I am very grateful for what you do. A librarian can really bring magic to a child's life through books.

Lastly, thank you to my readers. You have no idea how excited I get when I hear about you loving your adventures with Eleanor. My whole goal in writing these books was to give something for children to read, and I am so thankful for those of you who have found Eleanor. I'm so excited to hear what you think about City of Gold, and especially Fenek.

Always believe in Fairytales.

NIKKI MITCHELL is the American author of *Eleanor Mason's Literary Adventures*. Her debut novel, *Nightshade Forest*, was release in 2020, followed by *City of Gold* in 2021.

When she isn't writing and hanging out with her fictional friends, she is a stay-at-home mom and home-schooler to her two children, Evelyn and Everett. She is married to her high school best friend and loves spoiling her three cats, Gandalf, Bellatrix, and Ousque.

She lives in the Upper Peninsula of Michigan and is a Northern Michigan University graduate.

Nikki is an avid reader of fantasy and classics and collects special editions of *Fahrenheit 451* by Ray Bradbury and *Alice's Adventures in Wonderland* by Lewis Carrol.

Connect with Nikki on social media:
Instagram: nikkimitchellauthorpage
Facebook: Nikki Mitchell Author
www.eleanorsliteraryadventures.com

ALSO BY NIKKI MITCHELL

Nightshade Forest:

Book one Of Eleanor Mason's Literary Adventures

Letters from Eleanor are available for young readers by visiting www.eleanorsliteraryadventures.com and filling out the form.